THE
PARKER TWINS
S E R I E S

5

Secret of the Dragon Mark

THE PARKER TWINS SERIES

5

THE PARKER TWINS SERIES

Secret of the Dragon Mark

JEANETTE WINDLE

Kregel
Publications

Secret of the Dragon Mark

© 1996, 2002 by Jeanette Windle

Published by Kregel Publications, a division of Kregel, Inc., P.O. Box 2607, Grand Rapids, MI 49501. For more information about Kregel Publications, visit our Web site: www.kregel.com.

The persons and events portrayed in this work are the creations of the author, and any resemblance to persons living or dead is purely coincidental.

Cover illustration: Patrick Kelley
Cover design: John M. Lucas

ISBN 0-8254-4149-8

Printed in the United States of America

1 2 3 4 5 / 06 05 04 03 02

THE INFERNO

His hand explored the surface of the wood. It was hot—and growing hotter! The edges of the heavy door were already charred black. Justin stamped frantically as a long finger of flame crept along the wooden floorboards. He snatched the rubber mat and shoved it against the bottom of the door. It wouldn't stop the black smoke filling the air, but it might buy him a little more time.

His skin burned with the rising temperature. Sweat trickled down his face and chest. He straightened up and drew in a deep breath—then wished he hadn't! His lungs burned. Choking and wheezing, he rubbed sooty fists into his streaming eyes.

A weak cough sounded behind him, and he whipped around to see the old man, now conscious and slumped against a wall of the small room. "Go!" gasped the crumpled figure, waving one hand uselessly at the smoke still seeping around the door frame.

Go? If only he could! Rushing across the room, Justin stripped off his jacket, wrapped it around his fist, then smashed his fist through the window. *Come on!* he willed desperately *There's got to be someone out there!*

He heard none of the usual afternoon activity. No footsteps, no cheerful calls of passing shoppers, not even the swoosh of passing cars. The only sounds were the feeble coughing of the old man and a faint, ominous crackling behind the scant protection of the closed door.

"Jenny! Lieutenant Adams! Where are you?" he muttered hoarsely. He wanted to cry out for help. But any call for assistance would attract his enemies—his and the old man's. Enemies who would gleefully cut off this last chance of escape!

A loud explosion knocked him off his feet. Pulling himself back to the windowsill, he glanced down. A ball of blue flame joined the tongues of red and orange that licked hungrily from every opening in the building.

He threw the few feet of homemade rope out the window and looked down. Three stories below waited a solid slab of concrete. Still he had a chance, even if it meant broken bones. At least he would escape this inferno. But how could he abandon the old man to certain death?

Justin pressed his aching head in his hands. There must be an answer, if only he could think clearly! *Time!* he whispered desperately. *I just need more time!*

But there was no time left. Even as he lifted his head, Justin saw the trail of flame climbing this side of the wooden door— the only barrier that stood between them and the crackling furnace on the other side!

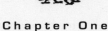

Chapter One

THE DEVLONS

"Oh, no! You've *got* to be kidding!" Justin's stack of homework slid unnoticed to the floor. He stared down the long corridor, dismay all over his face.

"Yeah, those soccer tryouts were sure tough!" Kneeling in front of a bottom locker, Jenny twisted the combination lock to the left, to the right, then back again to the left. "Of course, it makes a difference having a thousand kids in eighth grade instead of a hundred. I'll be lucky to make my class team, never mind the school . . ."

Jenny suddenly realized she'd lost her twin brother's attention. She glanced up, pushing back the heavy dark curls that had fallen over her face. "What's the matter?"

Justin jerked his head toward the far end of the hall. "See for yourself!" Dropping to his knees, he scrambled to pick up his scattered papers and books.

Jenny tugged at her locker door. When it didn't open, she turned her head to cast an absent glance down the long corridor. But she stiffened when she caught sight of the three boys who had come in a side entrance and were now swaggering down the hall.

"The Devlon cousins!" Her brown eyes flashed gold sparks. "They *would* have to end up here!"

It was their first day at Puget Sound Junior High. They had returned home from an adventurous summer to find that their southern Seattle neighborhood had been rezoned. The small middle school they'd attended for the last three years had been closed and their class scattered among several large junior high schools. The Parker's house fell right on the rezoning line, and to their disappointment, not one of their neighborhood friends had been transferred with them.

Just the Devlons! Justin thought gloomily, shoving his papers and books together into one untidy stack. The Devlons had been the neighborhood bullies since kindergarten.

He scooped his homework into his arms. "Come on, Jenny! Let's get out of here before they see us!"

But it was too late.

"Well, well. If it ain't the Parker twins!"

Justin lifted his head reluctantly. The Devlon cousins had stopped in the middle of the hall, nudging each other and pointing at them. Justin was tall and husky for his thirteen years, but all three of these boys were much broader and heavier. They looked curiously alike with shoulder-length, strawlike hair and bulging, pale blue eyes in round faces that had managed to sunburn and peel even in what passed for summer in the rainy Pacific Northwest.

The three cousins drew into a huddle, heads close together. Their muffled laughs and malicious glances gave Justin a sinking sensation in his stomach. This was shaping up to be a replay of similar scenes clear back to kindergarten, when the Devlons, already outweighing everyone else in the class, had snatched away the stickers Jenny had won for being the first to recite the alphabet. And only last year, they had cornered Justin behind the middle school gym and shoved a cigarette into his mouth. When he stubbornly refused to smoke, they followed him home on their bikes. After knocking him into an irrigation ditch, they rode off laughing, leaving him scraped and bruised with mud-soaked clothes, and a bent bike.

Justin hurriedly stuffed his homework into his backpack. He was no coward, but the last thing he wanted was to start the new school year with a fight! Slinging the backpack over one shoulder, he grabbed his soccer shoes. "Hurry up, Jenny!" he hissed. "What's keeping you?"

"I've got to get my homework, but my locker's stuck!" Jenny was almost in tears as she tugged again at her locker door. It wouldn't budge. She consulted the numbers scribbled on a scrap of paper in her hand, then ran through the combination again. "They *said* it was the right combination!"

Justin glanced down the hall. The Devlons had broken their huddle and were sauntering toward the lockers, their heavy footsteps echoing on the tile floor. Justin grabbed the scrap of paper from his sister. "Here. Let me try."

He twisted the combination lock right, left, and right again, then yanked at the door handle. It didn't move. Frustrated, he banged his fist against the locker. The door swung open.

"Would you look at that!" Justin helped his sister shovel the locker's contents into her backpack, then jumped to his feet. "OK! Let's go!"

But the Devlons were almost on them, grinning with

anticipated pleasure. The biggest cousin rubbed his man-sized hands together expectantly. Justin threw a worried glance over his shoulder. An hour earlier, school had been swarming with students, but Justin and Jenny had stayed behind for soccer tryouts, and now the hall behind them stretched empty and silent. Where was a teacher when you needed one?

Then a door slammed open halfway down the hall. A group of teachers poured out—the music faculty, judging by the instruments that several carried. The Devlon cousins backed off as the teachers surged toward the stairs, talking and laughing.

Justin grabbed Jenny's arm. "Here's our chance! Come on!"

Slipping through the group of teachers, they took the stairs at a run. They didn't slow down until they reached the main corridor of the school, still comfortably full of hurrying students and staff. Justin ran his fingers through his short, carrot-colored curls. "Man! That was a close one!"

The pair slowed to a more leisurely pace toward the wide, glass doors of the main entrance. "So, how were your classes?" Jenny asked.

Justin shrugged. "So-so. Tons of homework, anyway! Did you see anyone you know?"

"Nope." Jenny sniffed. "And not one person even said 'hi.' It's going to be a long year, at this rate."

"Yeah, I know what you mean," Justin grumbled. "You should—"

A shrill bell cut him off. Jenny stopped short and checked her watch. "Oops, that's for me. I'm going to be late!"

"Hey, where are you going?" Justin caught her arm as she turned away.

"I forgot I signed up for choir tryouts, too. See you at home." Adjusting her backpack to a more comfortable position, Jenny stretched her long legs into a half run down the corridor. But she'd taken only a few steps when she stopped and turned back.

"Oh, Justin!" she called. "Could you take these home for me? They'll get lost bumping around the choir room." She tossed him her pair of soccer cleats.

"Thanks!" Jenny waved a hand, then disappeared around a corner.

Justin tied the two sets of laces together and slung them over his shoulder. The black leather of the new shoes was still pretty clean. Dad had just gotten them for their fall soccer season, and they hadn't been cheap.

Yeah, it's going to be a long year. He frowned as he ran down the front brick steps. Nobody had been exactly friendly to him, either, except—well, there was that Asian boy who had sat next to him in a couple of his classes.

It had started when the math teacher gave Justin a simple algebra problem. Justin hadn't taken beginning algebra in his old school, and his answer set the whole class to snickering. It didn't help matters when the boy at the next desk proceeded to work out the problem with flawless ease. But when the teacher had moved on to another student, the boy had given Justin such a friendly smile that Justin couldn't help returning his grin. Later in English class, a grammar assignment had left the other boy completely baffled until Justin leaned over with a whispered explanation.

I didn't even ask his name! Justin hurried across the lawn to the bus stop at the edge of the school property. The school buses were all long gone; he'd just have to take the city bus. Easing his backpack to the ground, he checked the schedule posted on the end of a three-sided shelter that protected waiting passengers from the frequent rains.

"Well, well! Look who's here!" A heavy hand landed on Justin's shoulder. "If it isn't that Parker kid!"

Justin let out a silent groan. *Not again!* Slowly he turned around. A large chest covered with a skimpy T-shirt was only inches from his face. He raised his gaze to a pair of pale, fish-like eyes. He never could tell them apart, but this one looked like the biggest and oldest. He took a wild guess. "Hi, Arthur."

He was right! Arthur Devlon let his hand fall from Justin's shoulder. "'Hi, Arthur,'" he mimicked in a falsetto. "Like you sound real glad to see me!"

Justin glanced around warily. Two more Devlons flanked Arthur. And this time there was no teacher around to distract them.

"Look, guys," he said shortly. "I don't want trouble. I'm just waiting for my bus, see?"

Arthur's round face took on a wounded expression. "Hey, who said anything about trouble? We're just trying to be nice. Right, guys?"

The three cousins exchanged malicious grins.

Arthur stepped forward, forcing Justin back against the metal side of the bus shelter. Shoving his plump face close to Justin's, he poked him in the chest with one fat finger. "Why'd you run off back there? I mean, here we are, buddies from the old school and you act like we're poison. I'd say you owe us!"

He glanced around at his two cousins. "What do you say, guys?"

"Yeah, let's give it to him!" sneered one of the other Devlons.

"Now just a minute, Bill!" Arthur held up a beefy hand. He was smiling, but that didn't make Justin feel any better. "We don't want to hurt him—not on the first day. We just want . . . yeah, that's it, a present! I mean, he did forget my birthday this summer."

"Yeah, mine too!" Darting in from the side, Bill Devlon snatched at the two sets of cleats Justin carried over his shoulder. "These'll do for me."

"Come on, give those back!" Justin lunged for the shoes, but Bill Devlon danced out of reach.

"Does the little baby want his toys back?" he teased, holding the soccer shoes well above his head.

"Come on, Bill, you don't need two pairs!" Ben Devlon shouted. "Toss one over here."

"Hey, just a minute! I get first crack!" Arthur stepped back to snatch the shoes away from his cousin, leaving Justin momentarily free. Behind him, he heard the screech of air brakes. A bus was coming. Now would be the time to make a run for it!

But Justin was starting to boil inside. He'd done his best to avoid a fight, but no Devlon was going to walk off with his and Jenny's new soccer shoes! His jaw tightened. Through clenched teeth, he demanded, "Hand them over or I'll . . ."

"Or you'll what?" Throwing back their heads, the three Devlons laughed uproariously.

That did it! Justin's green eyes blazed with anger. Without warning, he dove for Arthur, butting him in his well-rounded middle. The bigger boy tripped, falling hard. Justin made a wild grab for the soccer cleats, but as his hand tightened around the laces, someone landed on his back. A moment later, all four boys were rolling on the grass.

Somewhere in the background, Justin heard the bus pick up speed and move away. Twisting and turning, he kicked and threw punches as hard as he could.

But it was three against one, and Justin was definitely getting the worst of it. His lips stung, and he could taste the salt of blood trickling into his mouth. A blow in the stomach knocked the breath out of him. Someone's backside landed on his chest, and another heavy body sprawled across his legs. He was slowly suffocating.

"Ki-yah!" A bloodcurdling cry pierced the grunts and triumphant yells of the Devlons. Justin could suddenly breathe. He rolled over with a groan, keeping a cautious eye on his three opponents. But the Devlons had lost all interest in him. Sitting up, Justin turned to follow their slack-mouthed stares.

Leaping high into the air, a slightly built dark-haired boy kicked both legs out in front of him. Coming down on the balls of his feet, he whirled in a dizzying series of sidekicks.

Justin recognized the boy's round face and thick, black hair. It was the Asian kid from math class. But the black eyes no longer smiled.

"Cool!" Bill Devlon finally broke the silence, his eyes round with admiration and respect. "Was that kung fu, or what?"

He shrank back as the small figure flipped backward, then whirled around to face the three bullies. The Asian boy stood in a half crouch, his slim, brown hands held flat and stiff in front of him in a classic martial arts position. He hadn't come close enough yet to land a single kick or hit. But the three Devlons stumbled to their feet and backed away.

Taking advantage of their confusion, Justin snatched up the two pairs of shoes that now lay forgotten on the grass. Scrambling to his feet, he backed off to one side, but stayed close enough to jump in if his rescuer needed help. He grinned to himself to see the three bullies retreating from a boy who hardly reached their shoulders.

Arthur scowled. He motioned for his cousins to stop their retreat, then stomped forward. Planting himself in front of the other boy he sneered, "Bug off, kid! Or we'll take care of you next!"

The boy didn't answer. He stood balanced on tiptoe, his black eyes narrowed and watchful. His straight, black bangs flopped down into his eyes, but he didn't blink or move a muscle. Suddenly his lips curled back. He growled a low, warning growl.

"Come on, man!" Bill plucked nervously at Arthur's sleeve. "Can't you see the kid's some kind of martial arts freak? You don't want to mess with him. Let's get out of here!"

"You think I'm afraid of this . . . this *kid!*" The biggest Devlon brushed his cousin aside. "No way. Get him!"

"Ki-yah!" A shriek that froze Justin's blood sent Arthur stumbling back against his cousins. Throwing himself into another back flip, the small figure whirled in a dazzling display of kicks and hand chops that came within inches of Arthur's terrified face. Then he froze in a crouch, his dark eyes glaring dangerously at the three cowering Devlons. His hands curled rigidly in front of him. His lips drew back in a snarl. He looked like some dangerous jungle animal!

Chapter Two

A NEW FRIEND

It was too much for the Devlons! Turning as one, they ran until they had put half a block between themselves and their opponent. When they glanced back, the boy raised his hands in a threatening gesture.

The three bullies broke into a run. But Justin's rescuer didn't relax his watchful stance until they had disappeared around a corner. Then the curved hands dropped to his side. The glare faded from the black eyes. Suddenly he was just a skinny black-haired boy whose head barely topped Justin's shoulder.

Justin's green eyes sparkled. "Wow! You were awesome! What are you—a black belt?"

The other boy hunched his shoulders. To Justin's surprise, he looked embarrassed. "Well, I'm not really . . . I mean, I've never . . ." Thrusting his hands into his pockets, the Asian boy drew in a deep breath. "I'm not *any* kind of belt."

"What do you mean?" Justin demanded. "You mean you don't know martial arts? But I saw you—all those flips and kicks!"

The boy's face lit up with an impish grin. "Yeah, well, I learned tumbling in gymnastics. The rest . . . well . . . I watch TV! I used to play karate all the time."

The memory of the Devlons' scared red faces suddenly struck Justin as the funniest thing he'd ever seen. He began to laugh helplessly. After a moment, the other boy joined in.

The two boys were soon laughing so hard that they collapsed on the grass. Justin clutched at his aching side. "Did . . . did you see their faces when you growled?" he gasped.

"Yeah, my best 'Tony the Tiger' imitation!" the other boy managed to sputter. The two boys rolled back and forth in another attack of helpless laughter.

"Talk about weird!" Jenny stood over Justin, hands on her hips.

Justin sat up. "Jenny! I thought you had choir tryouts."

"They got cancelled," Jenny eyed the two still-giggling boys. "I thought *you* had a bus to catch."

"The bus!" Justin sprang to his feet. The #27 was turning the corner a block away. Justin quickly turned to the Asian boy. "Anyway, thanks. I owe you one."

Then he realized that he still didn't know his rescuer's name. "I'm Justin Parker. This is my sister, Jenny."

The other boy scrambled to his feet. "It's nice to meet you. I'm Danny Nguyen." Danny pronounced his last name Wing.

There was a screech of air brakes as the bus pulled to a stop in front of the shelter. Justin broke into a run.

"We'll see you around, Danny," he called back over his shoulder. "You sure saved me a beating!"

"What do you mean—a beating?" Jenny demanded as they hurried toward the bus stop. For the first time, she noticed his cut lip and grass-stained clothes. "Have you been fighting?"

"I'll tell you about it on the way home," Justin said, as they scrambled aboard the bus.

Justin didn't see much of Danny Nguyen over the next few days as they rushed from one class to the next so he was pleased to find himself in the cafeteria line behind the other boy on Friday. Danny looked just as pleased when Justin tapped him on the shoulder.

"So, how's it going?" Justin raised his voice above the clatter of trays and chattering students. "You don't seem to know anyone around here, either. Is this your first year, too?"

"Yeah." Danny set his tray down on the table. "My family just bought a restaurant near here. You from around here?"

"Hi, guys!" Before Justin could answer, his sister plopped her tray down beside him. Justin pointed across the table. "You remember Danny, don't you?"

"Sure!" Jenny gave Danny a wide smile as she slipped a straw into her chocolate milk. "The Japanese black belt who rescued you from the Devlons."

"Hey, do I look Japanese?" Danny drew himself up straight, looking as offended as possible. "I'm from Vietnam!"

Jenny was taken aback. "Sorry! I didn't mean . . ."

"It's okay." Danny stabbed at a soggy piece of hamburger bun. "It's just that Vietnamese don't appreciate being called Japanese or Chinese any more than you'd like me calling you a Russian or Irish."

"I never thought about it that way," Justin admitted. "I mean, about all those Asian countries being that much different."

Like all of Seattle, Puget Sound Junior High was a melting pot of every nationality. Justin knew that many students came from families who had immigrated to the United States. But he didn't know much about Vietnam, except that the United States had fought a long, drawn-out war there before he was even born.

Justin had a dozen questions he wanted to ask, but he didn't know if Danny would mind. As usual, Jenny didn't hesitate. She leaned forward eagerly. "So how long have you lived here? Do you miss Vietnam? How'd you get an American name?"

"Hey! One at a time!" To Justin's relief, Danny laughed at Jenny's curiosity. He latched on to her last question. "My name's really Nguyen van Dien with the last name first, see? The immigration officer nicknamed me Danny. That's what *Ông Nôi* says, anyway."

"*Ông Nôi?*" Eyebrows arched, Jenny struggled to pronounce the unfamiliar words—umg noy. "What's that?"

"Not *what—who. Ông Nôi* is Vietnamese for 'Grandfather.' I don't remember Vietnam. I was only a baby when we came here. I'm American now, just like you."

"So that's why you speak such good English!" Jenny said with satisfaction. "Do your parents speak English, too?"

Danny's impish grin suddenly disappeared. "I don't have any parents. They died in Vietnam."

"Oh! I'm so sorry," Jenny stammered. "That . . . that's awful!"

"Hey, don't worry about it," Danny said quickly. "It was a long time ago. I don't even remember them. It was my grandfather who brought me here to America."

Jenny's brown eyes were sympathetic. "I can't imagine coming all that way to a strange country. Your grandfather must be very brave!"

Danny shrugged. "I don't remember anything about it. *Ông Nôi,* though—he's got some stories you wouldn't believe!"

He sat up straight with sudden excitement. "My house is just a few blocks away. Why don't you come over after school today. I'll get Grandfather to tell you some of his stories."

But his excitement drained away when the two exchanged a doubtful glance. He pushed back his plate, his face carefully expressionless. "Never mind. It was a dumb idea."

"No, wait—we'd love to meet your grandfather. It's just . . . we've got to ask Mom and Dad first."

"Of course!" Danny nodded politely, a smile once more lighting up his dark eyes.

"Does the little boy have to ask Mommy before he can play with his friends?" The sneering drawl fell into a momentary lull in the lunchroom chatter.

"The Devlons!" Justin didn't need Jenny's hiss to guess who was behind him. A wave of red rose to the roots of his carrot-hued hair as he caught the hooted comments from a nearby table. But he looked squarely up at Arthur and answered clearly, "Sure, I ask permission. My parents don't take off without letting me know where they're going, and neither do I."

Muffled snickers broke out around him. Justin tensed as the biggest Devlon clenched his fists. But one of his cousins tugged on the bully's sleeve. "Hey, Art! There's that kid!"

Art Devlon's pale eyes rounded fishlike as he caught sight of Danny calmly eating on the other side of the table. The three cousins backed hastily away. Jenny giggled as they disappeared almost at a run into the maze of tables. "They're going to be pretty mad when they find out the trick you guys played on them!"

"We won't tell if you don't!" Justin assured her, exchanging a conspiratorial wink with Danny. Pushing back his chair, he threaded his way to the nearest telephone booth.

But when he told his mother of Danny's invitation, she said firmly, "Justin, you know our family rule. We want to meet your friends before you go visit in their homes."

"Aw, Mom!" Justin groaned. "He's a really nice guy."

"I'll tell you what," Mom suggested. "Why don't you invite Danny over here for the night—let us get to know him."

Hurrying back to the table, Justin told of his mother's suggestion. Now it was Danny who hesitated. "I'd really like to, but . . . well . . . I've got to call my grandfather first!"

The three children looked at each other, then burst out laughing.

"Danny," Justin assured him solemnly, "I think my parents are going to like you."

Danny's grandfather gave him permission to spend the night with the Parkers. As Justin predicted, both his parents were impressed with Danny's politeness. The Parkers couldn't help laughing at his expression when he tasted the stuffing at dinner. Later, he asked Justin seriously if his mother always filled her chickens with wet bread!

Danny ducked his head with awkward embarrassment when the Parkers bowed their heads to bless the food. But he listened with interest during family devotions the next morning. When Dad asked if anyone had a question, he asked hesitantly, "Is this God you read about the same Jesus who was born in a manger?"

Dad beamed. "So you know the Christmas story! Yes, God became a man when Jesus was born."

"Yeah, I saw the story on TV once. But my grandfather made me turn it off." Danny sounded regretful.

It was the next Friday before Justin and Jenny could accept Danny's invitation to meet his grandfather. After soccer practice—both twins having made their class teams—they set off, following a map Danny had sketched.

The narrow streets surrounding Puget Sound Junior High were a far cry from the Parker's own prosperous neighborhood. The buildings were made of brick and badly in need of repairs and a fresh coat of paint. The twins had been walking some fifteen minutes when they turned a corner to find themselves on a wider street lined with small businesses and restaurants. The signs on storefronts and windows didn't look like any writing the twins had ever seen. Some of the businesses had English translations under the oriental characters—Nam Hoa Styling Salon, Vien Van Toc Jewelry, Thuc Pham An-Hing Grocery. Most of the hurrying shoppers were of Asian descent.

Jenny paused to peer into the grocery window, wrinkling her nose at the squid and octopus tentacles displayed on blocks of ice. Crossing another street, the twins found themselves in a wide, vacant lot. The empty lot was not paved but had been smoothed off to use as a parking lot, and beside the lot was a square, three-story brick building.

Jenny consulted the map. "That's it—La Vie Restaurant!"

The front door of the restaurant was glass with a stylized dragon painted on it. Before the twins could knock, the door swung open with the faint tinkling of a bell. Danny waved them inside. "Well, here it is, guys! The best Vietnamese food in Seattle."

Justin looked around. He wasn't sure what he'd expected—maybe something of the ornate decoration he'd seen in Chinese restaurants: red carpets, black lacquered furniture, gilt-edged mirrors. But the furnishings here were simple, square, wooden tables scattered around one big room. The only touch of color was added by a large silk and bamboo fan painted with an exotic country scene. A row of booths ran along the far side of the room.

Justin glanced up. "I know it isn't much," Danny said, with a defensive lift of his shoulders. "But we're working hard. Someday this is going to be the most famous Vietnamese restaurant on the West Coast."

"Oh, I think it's great!" Justin assured him hastily, and Jenny added, "It's not fussy. I like that."

The restaurant was empty except for one man who was scrubbing a nearby table. The man was tall for a Vietnamese and strongly built. At first, Justin thought he must be Danny's grandfather. Then he realized that this man was still young, perhaps in his late twenties. He continued scrubbing as the three children walked across the restaurant, but Justin felt the man's eyes watching them through coarse, shoulder-length black hair.

"You missed a spot there!" Danny pointed out cheerfully as they passed the table. He added a comment in what Justin guessed to be Vietnamese.

The man made no answer. Raising a broad, dark face, he gave Danny a long, unsmiling look. Justin noticed his left eyelid twitch twice. Something in the expressionless, black eyes made Justin look away quickly. He was relieved when the man went back to scrubbing tables.

"That's Hue," Danny informed the twins as he led them

toward a counter that stretched across the back of the restaurant. "He works for us—cleaning, washing dishes—all that stuff. He's not much of a worker—always sneaking off. I guess *Ông Nôi* would fire him if he wasn't a cousin of ours."

Jenny grimaced. "I don't think he liked us very much."

"Oh, Hue doesn't like anyone," Danny said. "He can speak English if he wants to—he's been here several years now. But he won't."

Leading Justin and Jenny behind the counter, he pushed open the swinging door that led to the kitchen. "Let's see if we can talk *Ông Nôi* into a glass of *trai nhan-long ap*."

"Of what?" Justin demanded.

Danny laughed. "You'll see."

The kitchen was crowded and hot, but empty. Danny glanced around, puzzled. "Now where did he go? He was in here when I went to do my homework."

Justin sniffed at several large pots that bubbled on a huge stove. The aromas reminded him how long it had been since lunch. Opposite the gas stove was a long, flat cooking surface for stir-frying vegetables and meat. The deep-fryer crackled with fat. A commercial dishwasher and an enormous sink stood by a door that led to the back parking lot.

"*Ông Nôi's* worked here ever since we came from Vietnam," Danny said. "For years, he saved every penny he could. This summer he bought out his boss. That's when we moved out here."

"So where did you live before you moved here?" Jenny asked curiously. "Do you miss it . . . and your old school?"

"Not hardly," Danny grimaced. "We were living down in . . ."

The twins recognized the district he mentioned as one of the more run-down areas of inner-city Seattle, known for its gang wars and delinquency.

"We had a one-room apartment with plumbing that didn't work half the time. *Ông Nôi* hardly let me set foot outside except to the school bus and back. While the other kids were out throwing around a basketball—and getting into trouble—I was inside studying. And there were no other Vietnamese. We were down here more than at home anyway with the hours *Ông Nôi* put in. That's where I learned my gymnastics—from a Chinese trainer down the street where *Ông Nôi* used to park me after school while he was working. No, I was glad to move."

The tinkle of a bell interrupted Danny's explanation. He sprang to open the back door. An elderly Vietnamese man wheeled in a bicycle piled high with bundles. Grabbing for the bicycle, Danny lifted off a stack of bundles.

"*Ông Nôi!*" he scolded. "You've been doing the deliveries again. You promised to let Hue handle them."

His grandfather answered in rapid Vietnamese, and Danny switched to that language. Justin eyed Mr. Nguyen curiously. Not much taller than they were, he wore short-cropped hair and a long, drooping mustache streaked with gray. Danny dressed like any other American teenager, but his grandfather wore a long, high-collared black shirt over tight, black pants that reached only to his ankles.

Danny's grandfather broke off his flow of Vietnamese as he caught sight of Justin and Jenny. Peering through thick, black-rimmed glasses, he said softly, "Danny, will you introduce me to your friends?"

Mr. Nguyen bowed as Danny introduced them, looking over their heads into the distance. He didn't smile, but his deeply lined face was kind. "You are welcome here, friends of my grandson," he said solemnly.

Mr. Nguyen's English was good, but it had a singing lilt that Danny's American-grown speech lacked.

Danny returned to his earlier argument with his grandfather. "Why don't you let *me* do the deliveries? I can stay home from school until you get some help."

"No! I will not have my grandson grow up to know nothing but this!" Mr. Nguyen indicated the hot kitchen with a quick, chopping gesture. "This is America, where a man may be anything he likes. But only if you study!"

Glancing sideways at the twins, he added with simple pride, "My grandson is a very good student. He is going to be a doctor—like his father and mother before him."

Danny looked embarrassed, but he refused to change the subject. "You could at least get a car to do the deliveries. It would take you half the time as that old bike, and you wouldn't get so tired. You aren't so young anymore, *Ông Nôi!*"

"A car!" Mr. Nguyen almost snorted as he lifted an armful of packages to the counter. "The Vietnamese have always used bicycles. It is the way we do things."

"But we're Americans now," Danny protested. "A car is the American way."

"American ways!" his grandfather answered contemptuously. "They do not know proper respect! Vietnamese children do not question their elders." But his dark eyes rested affectionately on his grandson.

He gave Danny a push. "Enough! Where are your manners? You have not served your friends refreshment."

The twins soon found out what *trai nhan-long ap* was. "It's called logan fruit in English," Danny told the twins.

The three carried their tall glasses into the restaurant. Justin looked around for the man Danny had called Hue, but the big room was empty. Sliding into a corner booth, he sipped his drink cautiously. The logan juice was pretty good, but Justin wasn't so sure about the white, grapelike loganberries at the bottom of the glass. They were chewy with a taste something like a cantaloupe.

Justin paid little attention to the front doorbell until Mr. Nguyen hurried out from the kitchen. Danny pushed back his glass. "I'd better go help my grandfather. The restaurant will be filling up pretty soon."

"Can we help with something?" Jenny asked.

"No, you stay here and look through the menu. I'll get *Ông Nôi* to make whatever you want for supper." Danny slid to the edge of the booth. Suddenly he stopped. "What the . . ."

Justin glanced up at Danny's exclamation of dismay. "What's the matter, Danny?"

But as he turned his head to look across the restaurant, he drew in a sharp breath. Mr. Nguyen stood frozen behind an old-fashioned cash register at the far end of the counter. But it wasn't the old man that drew Justin's horrified attention. It was the hooded, black figure that had somehow made its way across the big room without a whisper of sound.

The stranger stood over Danny's grandfather. Across his back was a dragon—a dragon unlike any Justin had ever seen. Its snarling mouth was as wide as its serpentine red-and-gold body. The flat eyes of the dragon glittered evil and cruel.

The hooded head turned toward the three friends. Justin's heart stopped when he saw that it had no face!

Chapter Three

MEN IN BLACK

The black figure moved. The glare of the dragon dissolved into the simple reflection of light on embroidery and sequins. The horrifying, empty face became a mask of silken material that covered all but the eyes.

It's just a man—a man in a black jumpsuit! Justin thought. He studied the masked figure with interest. The hooded jumpsuit was of the same silken material as the mask. A black sash around the waist and high black boots of soft leather completed the unusual dress.

Danny's grandfather opened the cash register. The masked man stood watching, one elbow propped on the counter. He carried no weapon and no longer seemed particularly frightening. Justin relaxed against the side of the booth. *Just some guy in a martial arts outfit!*

But when he turned to make a relieved comment to Danny, Justin stiffened. The Vietnamese boy was still staring at the black figure, his eyes narrowed into slits. Turning, Justin saw Mr. Nguyen's hands tremble as he counted out a fat stack of bills.

The masked man looked down at the stack, then up again at Mr. Nguyen. The man in black didn't say a word, but Justin found himself shrinking back inside the booth. The old man hastily pulled several more bills from the cash register and added them to the stack. The figure in black still didn't move. Mr. Nguyen added more until the masked man snatched up the money. Without a sound, he glided toward the door.

Danny was across the big room before the front door shut, Justin and Jenny at his heels. He rushed behind the counter to his grandfather's side. "*Ông Nôi,* how much did he take this time?"

Mr. Nguyen looked old and frail as he replaced the few remaining bills with shaking hands. Justin didn't understand his muttered Vietnamese, but Danny crashed his fist down on the counter. "How did he know? How does he always know how much we've made?"

Justin and Jenny stared from Danny to the old man. "You mean that guy stole all your money?" Justin couldn't believe his ears. Scrambling onto one of the tall bar stools, he rested his elbows on the counter. He shook his head in confusion. "But . . . but he didn't even have a gun!"

"He doesn't need one!" Danny said savagely. "If we don't give him what he wants, he'll come back with ten more like him!"

"But . . . who *was* he?" Perching on another stool next to her brother, Jenny leaned forward across the counter. "Why was he dressed like that?"

Mr. Nguyen was silent, his thin hands shuffling through the almost-empty cash register. It was Danny who explained with obvious reluctance, "He's a member of the Dragon Tong."

"Tongs?" Justin pictured the long set of pincers his mother used to serve salad.

"No, a *tong!*" Danny said impatiently "It's a kind of secret organization—like the Mafia. The Dragon Tong showed up around here a few months ago, just after we moved. No one knows who they are behind those black masks, but they all wear that dragon on their backs."

"But what do they want?" Jenny asked. "Why are they taking your money?"

"They *say* they're here to protect the Vietnamese businesses from robbers and gangs," Danny answered bitterly. "But the only protection we need is against the Dragon Tong!"

"We thought we would find peace in America!" Mr. Nguyen looked up suddenly, his eyes bleak behind the black-rimmed glasses. "But even here the tong prey on the Vietnamese people."

"But, what about the police?" Justin demanded.

"The police will not help us!" Mr. Nguyen's voice was sharp. "There is little difference between the tong and the police! And the hand of the Dragon Tong is everywhere! They do terrible things to those who call in the police."

Danny nodded. "*Ông Nôi's* right. They'd come in and wreck the place if we called the cops—burn it down or something. This restaurant's all we have!"

"But the police could stop them," Justin argued. "That's their job."

"No!" The sudden crack of Mr. Nguyen's open palm on the countertop made them jump. "The Vietnamese people do not need the help of outsiders. There will be no police! We will speak no more of this!"

Slamming the cash register shut, he disappeared through the swinging doors. There was an awkward silence as the three teenagers stared at each other. Justin slid off his stool. "We'd better go home."

"Please don't go! You haven't even eaten." Danny moved to block their departure. "*Ông Nôi* didn't mean anything. He was just upset about . . . about everything." He glanced anxiously from one twin to the other. "You aren't mad at me, are you?"

They exchanged a quick glance, then Justin shook his head. "Of course we're not mad."

"We'd like to stay—if you really want us to," Jenny added.

They followed Danny back to the corner booth, and he helped them order from the menu. Justin glanced around. The restaurant was filling up with Vietnamese customers now. The restaurant worker, Hue, had reappeared and was waiting on tables.

Soon Danny brought out three large platters of *Banh Xeo*—a giant omelet stuffed with pieces of pork, shrimp, bean sprouts, and other vegetables. The three teenagers were soon chattering and laughing, but Justin couldn't help noticing the faraway look in Danny's eyes when he thought they weren't looking.

"*Ông Nôi's* so sure I'm going to be a doctor!"

Danny's interruption cut right into one of Justin's jokes. He broke off in surprise. "What's the matter, Danny? Don't you want to be?"

"More than anything in the world!" the Vietnamese boy said fiercely. "*Ông Nôi's* counting on the restaurant to pay for college. But with the Dragon Tong taking everything we make . . ."

Danny hunched his thin shoulders. He seemed to have forgotten his two companions. "How *can* they know exactly how much we've made? It doesn't make sense!"

"What do you mean?" Justin pushed away his food. He'd suddenly lost his appetite. "What difference does it make how much you've made?"

"It makes a lot of difference. The Dragon Tong takes forty percent of everything the restaurant brings in. What's left doesn't even cover the cost of running this place! Every month *Ông Nôi* has tried to pay them less, but they always know exactly how much money the restaurant has made."

"But who could have told them?" Jenny let her fork fall to the platter, her brown eyes wide with distress. "I mean, they had to find out from someone!"

Danny shrugged. "*Ông Nôi* is the only one who handles the money, and he keeps the books locked up tight. There's no way anyone could have seen them! Unless . . ."

Danny broke off. Glancing from one anxious face to the other, he forced a smile and changed the subject. "Hey, Justin, you never finished your story about the Devlons and the spelling bee."

It was one of the few occasions where the Devlons had ended up looking like idiots instead of Justin and Jenny. After a moment's hesitation, Justin took up the story where he'd left off. Arthur Devlon's misspelling of a certain furry mammal as "b-a-r-e" had even Danny roaring with laughter, and for the rest of the meal no one mentioned the Dragon Tong.

They caught only brief glimpses of Mr. Nguyen scurrying between the kitchen and the cash register. But when they rose to go, he hurried over to the front door. The elderly Vietnamese made no reference to the events of the afternoon. But when Justin and Jenny thanked him with an awkward bow, he bowed back, a faint smile glinting behind the black-rimmed glasses. "You two are good children—obedient and respectful. You are welcome here anytime!"

"Sounds like a version of the old 'gangster' protection racket. 'You pay me to protect you, and maybe I won't wreck your business!'" Dad commented later that evening. "I've read about the tongs—secret organizations that have run criminal activities in Asian countries for hundreds of years. Someone has obviously set up their own version of the tongs here in Seattle to terrorize the Vietnamese people."

"So why don't the police stop them?" Jenny demanded. "I mean, how can they just let them steal from those people?"

Stretching out in his armchair, Dad ran long fingers through hair as red as Justin's. "It doesn't sound like your Vietnamese friends *want* police help."

Mom glanced up from her notebook where she was scribbling ideas for a new article. "Maybe you two should have a talk with Doug Adams."

Lieutenant Doug Adams was a longtime friend of the Parkers and a lieutenant in the Seattle police department. He was also the leader of the youth ministry at the church they attended. That Sunday the youth group was meeting at the Adams' log home after the evening service.

"Yeah!" Justin snapped his fingers. "That's a great idea, Mom! I'll bet he'd know what to do."

On Sunday evening, Justin and Jenny hung back until

Lieutenant Adams had waved the rest of the youth group out the front door. "Could we talk to you—in private?" Justin asked in a low voice.

Doug Adams was tall and broad-shouldered with dark brown hair chopped in a military cut. He didn't look at all like Justin's idea of a Korean. But the twins had often heard the story of how the police sergeant had come to the United States.

The son of a Korean girl and a young American serviceman who had died in combat, he had been found crying on a street corner in Seoul, the South Korean capital. Rescued and placed in a mission orphanage, he was adopted by a loving Christian couple who had longed for a son of their own, one of many half-American, half-Korean children who had found a home in the United States.

Lieutenant Adams' brown eyes crinkled at the corners as he took in their serious expressions. "Why the long faces?" he teased. "Have the two of you come to report a bank robbery?"

They exchanged a startled glance.

Lieutenant Adams' keen gaze suddenly narrowed. "Sure, we can talk."

He ushered them into his office. Pushing forward two chairs, he cleared a spot to perch on a corner of his desk. "OK, what's bothering you two?" The tall policeman listened without interruption as they told about their visit with the Nguyen family and described the black figure with the red-and-gold dragon.

"I figured you were just the person to help," Justin finished confidently. "I mean, they've got tongs and stuff in Korea, too, don't they?"

He was startled when Lieutenant Adams laughed. "Give me

a break, Justin! I was only three when I came to the U.S. That doesn't exactly make me an expert on Asian affairs!

"But . . ." He looked from one disappointed face to the other. "I *was* in Vietnam at the tail end of the war, and I *have* dealt a certain amount with the Vietnamese immigrants here in Seattle."

Their faces brightened immediately. Lieutenant Adams went on, "I've suspected for some time that a Vietnamese gang was operating in that neighborhood. But all I've had to go on were a few rumors. The problem is that the Vietnamese immigrants don't trust the police. You already found out that they aren't willing to report these crimes."

"But why not?" Jenny demanded. "It doesn't make sense! Don't they realize you're there to help them?"

Lieutenant Adams didn't answer. He sat silent for a moment. Then he asked, "How much do you two know about Vietnam and the war there?"

"Not much," Justin admitted.

Lieutenant Adams tapped the pencil against the palm of his hand. "Okay, then. The United States army had been helping the South Vietnamese army fight the Vietcong, a Communist rebel force. In 1973, the U.S. started pulling out of Vietnam. But the South Vietnamese army couldn't hold off the Vietcong on their own. Two years later, the Vietcong finally captured South Vietnam."

The police lieutenant's eyes were bleak with old memories. "When the Vietcong marched in, thousands and thousands of South Vietnamese fled the country. Anyone with an education—government leaders, doctors, teachers—was considered a traitor and an American spy by the Vietcong. Those who could, fled the country, and a lot of them made it to the United States. Many of these early refugees already spoke English, and for the most part, they've made a successful life for themselves."

"But what about the ones who didn't make it out?" Justin demanded. "I mean, all the ones the Vietcong thought were American spies?"

The pencil snapped in two as Lieutenant Adams' long fingers suddenly tightened. Startled, Justin and Jenny jumped. The tall policeman dropped the broken pieces on the desk. He looked sheepish. "Sorry, kids. It's just that I was in Saigon when the last Americans left and the Vietcong arrived. I still see red when I think of what the Vietcong did there."

"But what *did* they do?" Jenny was at the edge of her seat. "I mean, they couldn't throw that many people in jail!"

"The Vietcong didn't bother with jail," Lieutenant Adams answered grimly. "They rounded up thousands who didn't make those last flights. Most were executed or sent to concentration camps. Hundreds of thousands more were forced into slave labor. Even now thousands flee every year by boat or through the jungle. Of course, if the police catch them, they are immediately executed."

"Boy! No wonder Mr. Nguyen and the other Vietnamese don't want to call the police." Justin's freckled face was thoughtful. "They must think the police here are just like the Vietcong back in Vietnam."

"It's not just that. The Vietnamese immigrants want the American people to think well of them. Most of these new refugees are from peasant families with little education or training. They are hard workers and are willing to take any kind of job to support their families. But there are always a few in any nationality who'd rather live at the expense of others. The Vietnamese are ashamed to admit that some of their people are criminals. That's one reason we haven't been able to confirm our suspicions about these gangs."

"But now you know there is a gang down there!" Justin was on his feet. "You could go right in and arrest them—maybe even tonight."

"Yeah, we could show you the way!" Jenny's heart-shaped face was lit up with eagerness. "We might even get Mr. Nguyen's money back."

"Hold it, kids!" Lieutenant Adams held up a warning hand. "I can't just walk in there and start making arrests. I mean, there *are* such things as evidence and witnesses."

"But *we're* witnesses," Justin protested. "We told you what we saw!"

"You saw Mr. Nguyen give some money to a man in a martial arts outfit," the tall lieutenant told them kindly. "The man wasn't even armed. And Mr. Nguyen didn't report any kind of robbery to the police. We're going to need more evidence than that— and more witnesses who are willing to testify against this gang. Until the Vietnamese people are willing to step forward and report those guys, our hands are tied."

Lieutenant Adams shook his head with genuine regret. "No, kids, I'm sorry. There's nothing I can do to stop the Dragon Tong."

Chapter Four

VIETNAM

"I guess that's it, then." Justin got to his feet, struggling to hide his disappointment. "Thanks for listening, anyway."

"Yeah, thanks." Jumping up beside him, Jenny did her best to smile.

"Look, kids. I'm sorry." Lieutenant Adams slid from his desk. "I know you want me to rush down there and arrest this Dragon Tong. But without hard evidence, I can't even convince my superiors that there *is* a gang operating down there."

Reaching across the desk he picked up the phone. "But I'll tell you what I *will* do. I'll have another patrol car assigned to that neighborhood. If we can catch this Dragon Tong in the act, we won't need a witness."

"Oh, thank you!" Jenny's disappointment evaporated. She gave the youth leader an impulsive hug.

"You're welcome," Lieutenant Adams said. Then he became serious. "By the way, there is something you can do."

"Us?" Justin and Jenny flashed each other doubtful glances. "What's that?"

"You can keep your eyes open and let me know the next time you see anything out of the ordinary. And encourage your friends to try trusting the police."

Lieutenant Adams started to dial, then stopped to give them a thoughtful look. "Has it occurred to you that maybe God brought you into Danny's life for a purpose? You may be just what it takes to break down that mistrust the Vietnamese community feels toward the police and bring the Dragon Tong to justice."

"Sure!" Justin's green eyes sparked with sudden excitement. "That's what we'll do. We'll talk Danny's grandfather into testifying. Then you can arrest that gang!"

It was the next weekend before they had another chance to visit Danny and his grandfather. The three teenagers had become close friends. Danny and Justin sat together in every class they shared, and the two boys joined Jenny every day for lunch.

"We'll get *Ông Nôi* to tell some of his stories," Danny promised when he invited them to spend Saturday at the restaurant. "This time nothing will go wrong."

"Yeah, right!" Justin grinned.

Jenny elbowed him sharply. "I can hardly wait," she assured Danny. "Maybe your grandfather will teach me how to make that yummy omelet we had last time."

They were up early Saturday morning and heading out the front door when Dad lowered his newspaper. "Just a minute, kids."

He tossed a piece of paper in their direction. "I thought this might interest Danny and his grandfather."

Justin picked up the folded sheet of paper. It was a church bulletin. "Hey, look, Jenny! The Carters are going to speak at our church tomorrow. Remember them? They stayed here the last time they were in the U.S."

"Yeah, I remember!" Jenny nodded. "They're the ones who showed that video of Cambodia and the refugee camps there."

"They were missionaries in Vietnam before the Communists took over," Dad commented, turning back to his newspaper. "They'll be talking about Vietnam as well as Cambodia tomorrow night."

"Cool!" Justin tucked the bulletin into his back pocket. "We'll invite Danny and Mr. Nguyen to come and hear them."

No one was in sight but Danny when they got to the La Vie Restaurant. "Hi, Justin—Jenny. Come on upstairs. *Ông Nôi*'s making some tea for us."

Danny ushered them up a wooden staircase at the back of the restaurant into a long, narrow room. The far end was empty. But near the door, a sofa and several mismatched armchairs were arranged around a low, black lacquered table. The floor was bare, but the floorboards were polished so Justin could see his Nikes reflected in the shining wood.

The room looked—somewhat to Justin's disappointment—much like any other American living room. Then he caught sight of the floor lamp that stood beside the biggest armchair. It was shaped like a dragon, and its huge, snarling mouth teased at his memory until he realized that this dragon looked much like the red-and-gold emblem he'd seen on the back of the masked man.

"Hey, Danny," Justin jerked his head toward the lamp. "I thought you said that was the mark of the Dragon Tong. What's it doing here?"

"Oh, this isn't just the mark of the Dragon Tong." Danny ran a hand over the red-and-gold coils that formed the base of the lamp. "This is a Vietnamese dragon. Our fairy tales have as many dragons as yours, only they don't have wings or breathe fire. They're more like giant sea serpents."

Jenny hurried across the room to where a bronze statue was displayed prominently on a small shelf just above her head. "Hey, Justin! You've got to see this!"

Justin studied the strange sculpture. The plump, squat figure sat with legs crossed, its jade eyes under a cone-shaped crown staring blankly across the room.

"That's Buddha," Danny explained. "The Divine One."

Jenny eyed the bronze image with undisguised horror. "You . . . you don't pray to that!"

Danny laughed. "Of course not! Only peasants believe in Buddha and the gods."

"What do you mean?" Jenny turned to stare at Danny. "Don't you believe in God?"

Danny shrugged. "We aren't religious. *Ông Nôi* doesn't like to talk about such things."

A knock at the living room door put an end to the discussion. Danny hurried to open it, and Mr. Nguyen entered, carrying a loaded tray. Danny took the tray from his grandfather. Mr. Nguyen turned to Justin and Jenny. Once again, he didn't meet their eyes as he greeted them with a solemn bow. But they now understood this was proper manners in the Vietnamese culture and a sign of respect.

Setting the tray down on the table, Danny poured tea into small, hand-painted china bowls. Mr. Nguyen passed around a plate of cream-filled pastries.

"These are delicious!" Jenny wiped her own fingers neatly on a napkin. "You sure are a good cook, Mr. Nguyen. Did you own a restaurant in Vietnam, too?"

"No, of course not! I was a teacher in Vietnam—a man of education." Mr. Nguyen sounded severe, but he heaped their plates with the cream-filled cakes.

Danny grabbed the last pastry as his grandfather set down the plate. "Please, *Ông Nôi*, won't you tell us about the war? Justin and Jenny would love to hear your stories."

"The war!" Mr. Nguyen gave a stern shake of the head. "To you, Danny, it is just an exciting story. To us, it was a terrible thing."

"Please, Mr. Nguyen," Jenny begged eagerly. "We'd love to hear how you came to America."

Mr. Nguyen settled back in his armchair, the glow of the dragon lamp accenting the deep lines of his thin face. Justin and Jenny both held their breath as Mr. Nguyen sat silent for a long moment, his eyes focused on faraway memories.

"The war was very bad," he began at last, his accented English rising and falling like a strange Asian melody, "but we did not suffer so greatly. We lived in Saigon, the capital, where there were many American troops to keep us safe from the Vietcong."

Mr. Nguyen looked down at Danny. "Your father—my son— was a son to make a father proud. So intelligent! So respectful! He studied hard to become a doctor. It was at the medical school that he met your mother. She was the first Vietnamese woman to finish the medical school. When they graduated, they were married."

Mr. Nguyen's gentle tones grew harsh. "Then came that terrible day! The Vietcong were everywhere! I knew that we should leave—go to America! But your grandmother and your parents didn't want to go. 'This is our country,' they said. 'We are needed here.'

"So we stayed, and the Vietcong came! Because my son and his wife had attended the Western medical school, we were called 'enemies of the state.' They took us to the jungle where there was not a village. We were told to build huts, to clear the jungle, to plant rice.

"My son and his wife were forbidden to practice medicine. The soldiers said they would contaminate the villagers with their 'Western ideas.' Every night there were classes telling us what we must believe. And always there were the soldiers watching . . . watching!"

There wasn't a sound in the living room except the old man's soft, accented speech. Though he must have heard the story many times before, Danny was listening as breathlessly as Justin and Jenny. Mr. Nguyen laid an affectionate hand on Danny's dark head.

"Nguyen van Dien—Danny—was born in that village. There were others who resisted and died, but we submitted. We learned to forget our city ways . . . to forget our education . . . to work, work, work in the fields. For my wife—Danny's grandmother— it was very hard, but there was Danny to think of. Only Danny's parents—they insisted on helping the villagers who needed them."

To Justin, Vietnam had never been more than a name. But as he listened spellbound, he began to see in his mind's eye the small village of thatched huts hacked out of the jungle. He could almost feel the blistering tropical sun as it beat down on the backs of the prisoners working long hours in the rice paddies. He shivered under the watchful glare of strutting Vietcong soldiers. He felt the fear and worry of the elderly Vietnamese couple when the young doctors slipped out under cover of darkness to help a sick villager.

Justin was so caught up in his own imagination that he didn't even notice that Mr. Nguyen had stopped talking until Jenny asked, "So what happened then, Mr. Nguyen? How did you get to America? What happened to Danny's parents?"

"The soldiers shot them," the old man said simply. "It was the day after Danny's first birthday. That was the day the soldiers came and shot my son and his wife."

"But . . . but why?" Tears were brimming in Jenny's gold-brown eyes. "Just because they were helping the villagers?"

Mr. Nguyen made a sudden, sharp gesture with his hand. "I do not wish to speak of it. It was done—that is all."

He added more gently. "It was long ago. I do not wish to make you sad, Jenny. Perhaps you do not wish to hear more."

"Oh, no!" Jenny ran a quick hand across her eyelashes. "Please go on."

"Yes, *Ông Nôi,* please!" Danny's own black eyes were shining with excitement. To him, the events of his early years were so long ago that they seemed only a thrilling adventure. "Tell us how you escaped."

Mr. Nguyen looked from one eager face to another. "As you wish. After . . . this happened, we—my wife and I—knew the time had come to escape. Not for us, but for Danny. We could not let this be the only life he would know."

The three teenagers listened wide-eyed as Mr. Nguyen told of the escape, wandering lost in the jungle with baby Danny strapped to his grandmother's back. Using the jewelry they had managed to hide from the Vietcong, the elderly couple bought a passage to freedom on a small fishing boat crammed with frightened refugees.

"We were twenty days at sea," Mr. Nguyen told them. "More than half the people on our boat died. Danny's grandmother—my wife—died only one day before a ship picked us up. The ship was from Hong Kong, and they took us to the refugee camps there. We were in the camps only one year. Because I had learned English as a teacher in Saigon, we were among the first to find a sponsor to bring us to America. We came to Seattle more than ten years ago. Here we have found a new home!"

They were silent when Danny's grandfather finished. Then Jenny impulsively got up and kissed the old man on the cheek. "Thank you, Mr. Nguyen, for telling us your story. I think you were wonderful to bring Danny all that way by yourself!"

"Yeah, that was pretty awesome," Justin added.

Mr. Nguyen looked pleased, but he only said, "I did what I had to do. I do not tell this story so that you may think well of me. I tell it for the thousands who are still in the camps, who are still trying to leave my country. Our story must be remembered! Perhaps one day all Vietnam will know freedom."

It was a wonderful day. At lunchtime, they learned to properly slurp up *Hu Tieu & Mi*—rice and egg noodle soup. Then Mr. Nguyen taught Jenny how to make fried rolls stuffed with shrimp and pork while Justin helped Danny deliver the hot rolls to several small cafés and delis in the neighborhood.

The three children were sitting at the counter, sampling the fried rolls and sipping a tall glass of *trai vay-ly chi,* another unfamiliar Vietnamese fruit drink, when Justin suddenly glanced at his watch. "Hey, Jenny, we've got to go. We've got that game tonight!"

The twins hurriedly drained their glasses and jumped down from the stools. Mr. Nguyen, a long apron around his neck and a large cleaver for chopping vegetables in one hand, stepped out of the kitchen to say good-bye. Justin was trying out his best Vietnamese bow when he remembered the invitation they had brought.

He pulled the church bulletin from his back pocket. "Mr. Nguyen, we'd like to invite you and Danny to come to our church tomorrow. My dad said he could come and pick you up. We've got some very special speakers coming we thought you'd like to hear. They used to be missionaries in Vietnam, and they're going to show a video of—"

"Missionaries!" The single, explosive word startled Justin. He stepped involuntarily backward as Mr. Nguyen snatched the bulletin from his hands. The elderly Vietnamese scanned the piece of paper, a growing anger on his thin, lined face.

"That's right, missionaries." Justin was puzzled by the old man's strange reaction, but he explained, "Missionaries are people who go to other countries to teach about Je—"

"I know what missionaries are!" Mr. Nguyen interrupted again. Crumpling up the bulletin, he threw it on the floor. His hand tightened on the cleaver. "You are friends of these— missionaries? You belong to their church—their religion?"

"Well, ye . . . yes." Justin stammered. "They're from our church. My parents have known them for years."

"Enough! Get out! Both of you!" Wide-eyed, they stumbled backward as Mr. Nguyen waved the cleaver. "Get out of my house! No friend of the Christian missionaries is welcome here!"

"But . . . but, *Ông Nôi!*" Danny pushed himself in front of the angry old man, his black eyes pleading. "Why? What have they done?"

"These *Christians* . . . ," Mr. Nguyen spat out the word as though it were filth, ". . . are no longer welcome here! It was the Christian missionaries who killed my son . . . who killed your parents!"

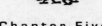

---------------- **Chapter Five** ----------------

THE APOLOGY

Justin never quite remembered how he and Jenny got out of the restaurant. Jenny's cheeks flamed with humiliation and anger as they hurried down the street.

"How could he throw us out like that?" she stormed. "What did we do to him?"

"Don't ask me!" Justin tilted his own hot face into the brisk September breeze. "I thought he liked us."

"I wonder what he meant." Jenny stopped suddenly to look at her brother. Hands on her hips, she demanded, "How could missionaries have killed his family? I thought he said soldiers killed them."

"Maybe he didn't understand all our English." Justin broke into a run as their bus pulled up to the curb. "We'll have to talk to Danny on Monday. Maybe his grandfather will have cooled down by then."

"It's probably just a misunderstanding," suggested Mom and Dad when the two explained why Danny and his grandfather wouldn't be coming to church with them the next day. Their sympathy comforted them, but the next evening Justin's thoughts kept sliding from the missionary presentation to the bizarre ending of their visit to the La Vie Restaurant. *Why did Mr. Nguyen get so mad? How could he possibly blame missionaries for killing his family?*

Oh, well. Danny'll tell us what's wrong tomorrow. Pushing Mr. Nguyen's strange behavior from his mind, Justin tried to pay attention to the colorful video of Vietnam and Cambodia.

But on Monday Danny wasn't in his usual seat. Looking around, Justin saw him hunched over a desk on the far side of the classroom. The Vietnamese boy glanced up, then quickly turned his head away.

Justin didn't hear a single word of the English teacher's lecture. At lunchtime, he threaded his way to the corner table where Danny sat alone with his meal. Setting down his tray he demanded, "Danny, what's going on?"

Danny shoved a folded piece of notebook paper across the table. Unfolding the note, Justin read its short message with growing anger. "What's this?" He crumpled the note. "We can't even talk? Why?"

Danny raised his head to look at Justin. His features were set and unsmiling. "I don't know," he said flatly. "I've never seen *Ông Nôi* so angry. But we can't be friends anymore!" Clamping his lips shut, Danny looked back down at his tray.

Justin picked up his own lunch and stomped away to the nearest table. "Fine! If that's the way you feel!" But as he glanced over his shoulder, he caught Danny watching him with eyes so full of misery that Justin softened. "It's OK," he said. "It isn't your fault."

That evening after supper, Justin and Jenny slipped downstairs to join their father in the basement. With Mom's birthday fast approaching, they'd plotted to build something Mom had dreamed of for a long time—her own office where she could retreat in peace to write articles and stories.

They'd started walling off one end for an office soon after Justin and Jenny's first visit to Danny's home. Mom was warned not to set foot on the basement stairs, and she carefully pretended she didn't know the significance of all the hammering and sawing downstairs.

"Here, son, take hold of that end."

Justin hurried to help his father lift the final section of Sheetrock into place. He reached for the bucket of nails, and hammered a nail through the Sheetrock into a stud. But his thoughts were far away.

"That's a hammer, Justin, not a crowbar!" his father teased, as Justin savagely yanked out another misplaced nail. Dad sang and told jokes as they worked, and didn't seem to notice how quiet his two helpers were.

"I wonder if those Dragon Tong guys ever came back," Jenny spoke up suddenly from the workbench where she was sanding wood for a computer desk.

"I guess we'll never find out now." Justin's freckled face was glum. They hadn't even gotten a chance to talk to Mr. Nguyen about letting Lieutenant Adams help the Vietnamese fight the Dragon Tong.

"What *are* you two talking about?" Like many twins, Justin and Jenny sometimes knew what the other was thinking. And since they often didn't even finish their sentences when they were talking together, outsiders—even their parents—tended to find their private conversations confusing.

Dad glanced from one teen to the other. "What's the matter, you two? Didn't you get things straightened out with Danny today?"

"We sure didn't!" Justin hammered in another nail with unnecessary force. "He won't even talk to us! His grandfather says we can't be friends anymore."

"He walked right by me this afternoon like I was invisible or something," Jenny added crossly. "I mean, it wouldn't hurt to be friendly!"

Dad laid aside his tools and sat on the workbench. "Remember, Vietnamese children are raised to obey their elders completely." There was a twinkle in his green eyes as he added, "A trait, by the way, that American children could stand to copy."

When they didn't respond to his humor, Dad sighed. "Look, I'm sure Danny would still like to be your friend. But he feels he must respect his grandfather's wishes. And he should."

"But it isn't fair!" Jenny lifted her small chin stubbornly. "We didn't do anything wrong. We just invited them to church! Why'd he get so mad?"

Dad put his arm around his daughter. "Jenny, from what you've told us, Mr. Nguyen is a kind and honorable man. He must have some reason for getting angry."

"Sure, he's got a reason!" Justin burst out angrily. Positioning the last nail against the Sheetrock, he swung his hammer over his head. "He doesn't believe in God, and he hates missionaries. Not to mention us!"

Justin brought his arm down with all the frustrated strength of his husky thirteen-year-old body. Before he could stop himself, the hammer had punched right through the wall.

Yanking the hammer out, Justin looked with dismay from the

jagged hole to his father. Dad stared back, one eyebrow raised in astonishment.

Jenny's sudden giggle broke the tension. "Wow, Justin! I didn't know you were strong enough to knock down a wall. You must be related to Samson!"

"Never mind, Justin," Dad answered. "I guess we didn't need to finish that wall tonight, anyway. Just pull out that section and set in another sheet."

Looking sheepish, Justin began pulling down the ruined section of the wall. Jenny turned back to her father. "So what should we do, Dad? Forget about Danny and his grandfather?"

"No, don't forget about them! We need to pray that God will change Mr. Nguyen's heart. Why don't we stop to do that right now?"

Justin felt better after they had prayed, but he wasn't at all happy during the next two weeks. Danny stayed far away and carefully avoided even looking in Justin's direction during class discussion. Justin now had other friends at school and on the soccer team, but they just weren't Danny. His only consolation was that Danny looked as unhappy as Justin felt.

The Devlon cousins, who'd left Justin alone while Danny was around, now bugged him every chance they could. Once, when the three bullies had him cornered in the hall, Danny walked by. Danny gave them a long, narrow stare, and the Devlons quickly scattered. Danny grinned briefly in Justin's direction before he hurried away.

By the end of two weeks, Justin had decided to accept the situation. So he was surprised to see Danny walk over to the table where he and Jenny were eating lunch.

"Hi, guys." Danny stopped beside the table. He didn't look too sure of his welcome, but he dropped into a chair and shoved a small, sealed envelope across the table.

Ripping open the envelope, Justin scanned the unfamiliar, spiky handwriting with astonishment. "Your grandfather wants to talk to us? But I thought he never wanted to see us again!"

"Here, let me see." Jenny snatched the envelope from his hand and quickly read the note. "He wants us to come today after school. Does this mean he's not mad anymore?"

Danny shrugged. "*Ông Nôi* doesn't explain anything to anyone. But, I don't think he's still angry." He looked across at them, eyes pleading. "I wouldn't blame you if you didn't come. But, I wish you would."

Justin and Jenny didn't even have to glance at each other. "Sure we'll come!"

"I'll call Mom and Dad," Justin added. "I know they'll let us go."

"Great! I'll see you at the restaurant then." Danny grinned, and then was gone.

The minute soccer practice was over that afternoon, they were off to Danny's at a run. But when they arrived hot and out of breath at the restaurant, there was no answer to their hesitant knock.

Cupping his hands around his eyes, Justin peered through the glass door. The big room that served as a restaurant was empty, but from somewhere inside, he could hear Danny's voice raised in anger. He knocked again, then tried the door. It was unlocked. Justin opened the door a crack, then pushed it open a little farther.

They'd just slipped inside when the kitchen door slammed open. The restaurant worker named Hue strode into the empty dining area. Danny stormed in behind him. "I heard *Ông Nôi* tell you to do those deliveries!" he said angrily. "Where were you?"

Ignoring the younger boy, Hue walked across the dining area with rapid, soundless steps. Justin, standing just inside the front door, noticed for the first time the athletic grace of the man's walk.

Danny stayed right on Hue's heels. "Where are you going?" he demanded sharply. "You take off any time you want and leave all your work to *Ông Nôi!* I don't know why he doesn't fire you!"

Hue didn't answer, but his black eyes glittered dangerously. Justin had time only to notice the rapid twitching of his left eyelid before the big Vietnamese pushed past them.

"Hue! Get back here right now!" Danny demanded.

"Enough!"

Danny whirled around at the sharp order in his grandfather's voice. The old man stood across the big room at the foot of the stairs that led up to the Nguyen family's living quarters.

"But, *Ông Nôi,*" Danny protested, as Hue disappeared through the door. "You aren't going to let him get away with this!"

"I have said 'enough!'" Mr. Nguyen turned to the twins. "You are welcome, Justin—Jenny. Danny, will you bring the tea while I show our visitors upstairs?"

Danny's scowl vanished when he saw his friends. "Justin! Jenny! You came!" Hurrying to their side, he urged them over to the foot of the stairs. "You go on upstairs. I'll bring the tray."

Justin and Jenny exchanged an apprehensive glance, but they followed the old man upstairs to the living room. Motioning them to the sofa, Mr. Nguyen seated himself straight and stiff on the edge of an armchair. The old man didn't say a word. Folding his hands in his lap, he gazed over their heads at the far wall.

Justin shifted uneasily as the silence dragged on. Mr. Nguyen had invited them over here to talk. So why didn't he say anything? He was relieved when Danny finally came through the living room door, carrying the tray. Now they'd find out what was going on.

But Mr. Nguyen waited until Danny had poured out four steaming bowls of tea before he broke his silence. "I wish to apologize. I have behaved badly to my grandson's friends. Will you forgive me?"

"Sure!" Justin and Jenny said at the same time. Scooting to the edge of the sofa, Jenny set down her tea bowl. "We're sorry we upset you, Mr. Nguyen. Does this mean you don't mind anymore that we're Christians?"

Mr. Nguyen didn't answer, but there was a glint of a smile as he said softly, "I have not asked you two here only to apologize; I wish to tell you a story. A story I have told no one else, not even my grandson. I did not want him asking questions about the Christian faith."

The three teenagers stared at each other, Danny looked as astonished as the twins. Taking off his glasses, Mr. Nguyen polished them carefully with a handkerchief, then settled them again on the narrow bridge of his nose.

"I have told you that my son and his wife came to know the Christian missionaries. Soon they went to their meetings and studied the Bible of the Christians. I did not like their friendship with these foreigners, but I said nothing."

Danny sat up straight. "You mean, my parents were Christians? Like Justin and Jenny? But, why . . . ?"

The old man looked displeased. Cutting Danny off with a sharp wave of the hand, he went on, "One day, my son and his wife came home to tell me that they had—how do you say it?—accepted Jesus as their Savior. After that it seemed that they talked of nothing else but this Christian God and His Son, Jesus Christ. Even my wife became one of these Christians. I did not like it, but the Christian missionaries seemed to be good people, and my wife and children were happy, so I said nothing. Until the day the Vietcong came to Saigon!"

The old man kept his voice even and his lined features expressionless, but Justin saw his gnarled hands tighten on the sides of the armchair. "If my family had not followed the Christian God, they would have listened when I told them we must leave. But they said they could not leave their church. They said they were needed to tell others about this Jesus!"

Justin sensed the old man's anger rising as he went on, "Religion was forbidden by the Vietcong. 'Help those who are sick,' I told my son, 'but keep quiet about this Jesus.' But even in the village with the soldiers watching everywhere, they could not stop talking about their God, praying with those they went to help. And one of those they helped betrayed them!

"The soldiers came. They found the Bible in our house. I covered my grandson's eyes as the soldiers shot his parents, and I cursed the day the missionaries had brought their Christian teaching to Vietnam!"

The three teenagers sat motionless as Mr. Nguyen finished. There was a long silence before the old man spoke again.

"When you spoke that day of the missionaries, I became very angry. Because of Christian missionaries, Danny will never see his parents again! But my anger should not have been turned against you. I have seen how unhappy Danny has been."

For the first time Mr. Nguyen looked directly at Justin and Jenny. "I see that you, too, have been unhappy. You are good friends for Danny. Will you forgive me and once more be a friend to my grandson?"

"Of course we will," Justin replied quickly.

"We're sorry about your family," Jenny added gently. "But please don't blame the missionaries."

Justin added, "Yeah, Danny's mother and father must have loved God very much to preach even when they knew they were in danger."

"Enough!" Mr. Nguyen stood up abruptly. "I have told you this so that you will understand why I was angry. You are welcome here as friends of my grandson. But speak no more of your Christian religion. Now I must go."

Justin slumped back in his chair as Mr. Nguyen hurried from the room. *Boy, did I say the wrong thing!* Staring down at his hands, he realized that he held an untouched bowl of tea. But just then, his gloomy thoughts were interrupted by an anguished scream.

Justin sprang to his feet. Tea spilled down his jeans and onto the floor. Jenny and Danny ran to the window. Setting the bowl down hastily on the table, Justin hurried to peer over Danny's shoulder.

Across the street, a Vietnamese woman stood in the doorway of a small grocery shop, sobbing and wringing her hands. Justin's sharp eyes picked out a black-hooded figure outlined against the shop entrance.

Another hooded figure appeared—then another! Altogether a half dozen poured out of the shop. Two carried heavy wooden bats. Ignoring the woman's cries, they smashed the glass window front of the small shop. Justin saw the snarling dragon emblazoned across their backs.

The Dragon Tong!

Chapter Six

ATTACK OF THE TONG

The three teenagers watched appalled as the masked members of the Dragon Tong smashed the windows again and again. The Vietnamese woman made a protest, thrusting herself between the two men and her small shop. But one of the masked men knocked her off her feet with one sweep of his arm, and another dragged her screaming out into the street.

"Hey, that's Mrs. Trinh!" Danny exclaimed, recognizing the small, middle-aged woman. "I guess she missed her payment." He turned to Justin and Jenny. "She had to take her little boy to the hospital yesterday. Pneumonia."

Jenny's eyes widened with horror. "You mean, they're wrecking her store just because her kid is sick? That's awful!"

"Isn't anyone going to help her?" Leaning out the window, Justin scanned up and down the block. But except for Mrs. Trinh and the members of the Dragon Tong, the street was empty. The usual shoppers had disappeared.

"Well, I'm not going to stand around!" Balling his hands into angry fists, Justin started toward the door. He had to do something! "Come on, you two! If no one else is going to help, we will."

"No, wait! You can't go down there!"

Justin ignored Danny's urgent call. Bounding down the stairs, he ran across the restaurant. Jenny and Danny were at his heels when he reached the front door of La Vie.

Peering through the glass, he watched the masked men throw the contents of the store through the open door of the shop. Justin reached for the doorknob, but hesitated when he saw the long knives they carried.

With practiced speed, the members of the Dragon Tong sliced open cartons and stabbed through containers of milk and juice. Broken glass littered the street, and fresh fruits and vegetables lay trampled underfoot. The Vietnamese shop owner stood in the middle of the street sobbing and wringing her hands. The sight of her helpless despair made Justin square his shoulders. He pushed open the door.

Danny grabbed at his sleeve. "Justin! Are you trying to get us all killed?"

Justin brushed Danny aside. But as he stepped outside, one of the Dragon Tong members turned his head to stare across the street at the three teenagers in the doorway. Justin froze. He swallowed hard as the black figure started in his direction. A long knife gleamed in one gloved hand.

"Justin, are you crazy?" Grabbing her brother by the back of his T-shirt, Jenny yanked him back inside the restaurant. She gave her brother an exasperated look as Danny slammed the door behind them. "Danny's right! Don't you remember what Lieutenant Adams said? We're supposed to call him if we see something strange—not take on the whole Dragon Tong ourselves!"

"Good idea!" Justin started toward the telephone on the

counter. "This time we'll get the police here whether anyone wants them or not!"

"No!" Danny reached the counter an instant before Justin. Snatching up the telephone, he hugged it tightly to his chest. "You heard what *Ông Nôi* said. You'll just make it worse!"

"Come on, Danny." Justin forced himself to stay calm. "That lady's your neighbor. Are you just going to let them get away with this?"

"Yeah, and just because she couldn't pay!" Jenny stood by her brother. "It's not her fault her son got sick."

"You're not kidding!" Danny loosened his grip on the telephone.

Seeing that he was weakening, Justin pressed his argument. "Look, you said the Dragon Tong wouldn't hurt anyone as long as you all paid. But take a look out there! What if it was you or your grandfather who got sick? What if *you* were the ones who couldn't pay?"

"Please, Danny," Jenny coaxed. "No one's going to know who called the police."

Danny sighed and then put the phone down. "I guess you're right. Go ahead and call."

Justin snatched up the receiver. "We've got to hurry!"

"No! Do not call!" The sharp order cracked across the big, empty room as Mr. Nguyen stepped through the swinging door of the kitchen.

"But, Mr. Nguyen!" Justin would have protested further, but he was cut off by the shrill wail of an approaching siren. *Good! Someone else called the police!* Dropping the receiver, he headed for the front door.

The siren grew louder. By the time Justin reached the door, a black-and-white police car had screeched to a stop across the street. But there was no longer any sign of the Dragon Tong. The shop owner ducked back into her shop. The street was now empty except for the shattered bottles and smashed containers.

Two officers stepped out of the patrol car. Justin recognized a tall, burly officer.

"Hey, Justin!" Jenny peered over his shoulder. "Isn't that Sergeant Preston? Come on!" She pushed open the front door. "That must be the patrol car Lieutenant Adams said he'd send. Let's go talk to them!"

Justin glanced back at Danny, but Mr. Nguyen ordered with a sharp wave of his hand, "Danny! Go upstairs!"

Danny started reluctantly toward the stairs. Justin hesitated, but to his surprise, Mr. Nguyen said brusquely, "Go to these police, if you must. Only do not ask me or my grandson to speak."

Giving a relieved nod, Justin followed his sister outside. As they crossed the street, the two patrol officers strode over to the grocery store to speak with Mrs. Trinh.

"I can't understand a word she's saying!" Sergeant Preston grumbled to his partner when Justin and Jenny approached. "Look, Rodriguez, why don't you round us up some witnesses. I'll see if I can figure out this lady's story."

Officer Rodriguez, a wiry, dark-haired young man who looked even slighter than he was next to the barrel-chested Preston, started across the street. He stopped with a grimace to wipe broken eggshells from his boots, and Sergeant Preston called, "Try and get us an interpreter too, will you?"

"Uh . . . sir?" Justin said hesitantly as Sergeant Preston turned back to the store owner.

Glancing up, the burly policeman said, "Just a minute, kids. I'll be right with you."

Justin and Jenny waited impatiently while Sergeant Preston interviewed Mrs. Trinh. The tiny Vietnamese woman seemed reluctant to answer, and her black eyes darted uneasily from one side to the other as she spelled out her name and address in uncertain English.

Seeing that the coast was clear, shoppers began emerging from the cafés and businesses. They hurried down the street, carefully skirting the grocery store and police car. Justin saw Officer Rodriguez stop several Vietnamese shoppers, but whatever he was asking brought only emphatic shakes of the head.

At last, Sergeant Preston finished with Mrs. Trinh and strolled over. "Sorry to keep you two waiting so long." Giving them a friendly nod, he flipped to a fresh sheet of notepaper. "OK, kids, what've you got?"

Officer Rodriguez strode up as Justin and Jenny began to speak, their words tumbling over each other. "There were about six of them—all dressed in black with big dragons on their back. The dragon means they're members of the Dragon Tong. They're making all the storekeepers pay them money—poor Mrs. Trinh, she didn't have money to pay."

The two officers frowned.

"And *that's* why they smashed up her store!" Justin finished, and Jenny added breathlessly, "You *will* catch them, won't you?"

They waited expectantly for the police officers' reactions. But when Justin glanced up, he saw with a sinking heart that their faces were now hard and unfriendly.

Sergeant Preston looked across at his partner, who shook his head. "No one I talked to saw any of these so-called masked bandits. In fact, none of them seem to have seen much of anything."

Slamming his notepad shut, Sergeant Preston looked stern. "What kind of a story is this? The store owner here says it was a gang of teenagers who busted up her store—and they weren't from this neighborhood, either. She didn't recognize any of them, but she says they definitely weren't Vietnamese!"

"But that isn't true!" Jenny gasped.

Justin glanced around. But Mrs. Trinh had slipped away. He felt like screaming with frustration. "Don't you see?" he insisted. "They're all scared of the Dragon Tong. That's why they won't say anything!"

Sergeant Preston slid his notepad into his shirt pocket. "Look, kids, I don't know what you're trying to pull. But lying to a police officer is a serious criminal offense."

"Come on, Preston." Officer Rodriguez strode toward the patrol car. "We're wasting our time here."

"Wait!" Justin stepped in front of the two officers. "Lieutenant Adams knows about the Dragon Tong! He knows we're telling the truth!"

"You know Lieutenant Adams?" Sergeant Preston's stern expression thawed a little.

"Sure. He's our friend."

He took a closer look at Justin and Jenny.

"Hey, weren't you two with that bunch of church kids the

lieutenant dragged down to the station for a tour a couple of months back?"

They nodded. "We told him about the Dragon Tong," Justin added. "He said he'd have a patrol car assigned to this area."

"The lieutenant did tell us to keep a sharp eye out for trouble in this neighborhood," Sergeant Preston admitted. "But there's nothing we can do with the store owner and a dozen other witnesses swearing it was just a gang of kids."

The burly officer opened the passenger door of the patrol car. "Look, kids, if I were you, I'd go home and stay out of trouble. Need a lift?"

"No, thanks." Justin and Jenny shook their heads. "We're here with friends."

Sergeant Preston leaned out the window as his partner started the engine. "I'll tell Lieutenant Adams what happened. That's all we can do."

Justin felt sick as the patrol car moved slowly away from the curb. "Well, that's that!" he muttered savagely. "One more hit for the Dragon Tong!"

Glancing over at the grocery store, Justin saw Mrs. Trinh peering from the shadow of the doorway. She waited until the patrol car disappeared around a corner, then hurried outside and began gathering up her scattered merchandise. The twins made an attempt to help gather up the cans and few bottles that were unbroken. But when the shop owner snatched the items from their hands, angrily shooing them away, the teens started back across the street.

Halfway across the street, Danny suddenly appeared at their side. "So, how'd it go?" he demanded.

Justin didn't say anything. He just kicked a broken container of water chestnuts down the street.

Danny shook his head as they walked on toward the restaurant. "I told you it was no good calling the police!"

"Sure!" Justin's tone dripped with sarcasm. "When no one but us saw anything. Now the police think *we're* the ones lying!"

"Shhh!" Jenny's fingers dug painfully into Justin's arm.

"Wha—" Annoyed, Justin swung around. But he bit off his angry reply when he saw what Jenny was staring at with wide, startled eyes. A single black figure had emerged from an alley. Moving with powerful grace, the Dragon Tong member glided without a sound to where Mrs. Trinh was trying to salvage some of the smashed groceries.

The masked man loomed over the tiny shop owner. Justin felt sure this was the same Dragon Tong member he'd seen in the Nguyen's restaurant more than three weeks before. Danny stiffened beside him as the black figure uttered one short, harsh phrase in Vietnamese.

"What did he say?" Jenny whispered.

Danny's round face was grim as he translated. "He says, 'This time your goods, next time your store!'"

The masked head turned toward the three teenagers standing in the street. "Come on, guys!" Jenny cried. "Let's get out of here!"

Whirling, she dashed for the front door of the restaurant with the boys at her heels. Justin glanced back. Then he froze, one hand on the door handle. The masked man was walking toward them!

Justin didn't even have time to open the door before the black figure reached him. For one endless moment, the Dragon Tong member's gaze burned down into Justin's eyes. Then Justin's throat caught in a soundless gasp. For as he stared upward, unable to move a muscle, he saw the left eye behind the silken mask twitch—twice!

Chapter Seven

A PLAN DEVELOPS

Without a word, the masked man turned and glided away. Justin stared after him until the black figure disappeared around the corner of the restaurant and into the alley. He couldn't bring himself to move until Jenny opened the door and yanked him inside.

"Justin, are you nuts?" she demanded. "Why'd you stay out there?"

Danny pulled him farther into the restaurant. "Did he say anything?" he asked.

Justin shook his head as he followed the other two toward the kitchen. The dining room was still empty. He glanced up at the clock above the kitchen door. It didn't seem possible that only an hour had passed since they'd arrived at the restaurant.

Danny pushed open the swinging door. His grandfather was standing at a long counter, chopping a steady stream of vegetables so fast the flickering movements of the knife could hardly be seen. "You should see Mrs. Trinh's store, *Ông Nôi!*" Danny announced. "There's food all over the street. They must have dumped everything in the place."

"So!" Mr. Nguyen didn't even look up. Pushing aside a mound

of onions, he reached for a slab of beef. "She should not have been so foolish."

"You don't mean that, *Ông Nội!* It isn't her fault her son was sick!" Danny unconsciously echoed Jenny's words.

"Perhaps not." Mr. Nguyen chopped even faster, as though the Dragon Tong itself were under his knife. "But she has lost everything. How will she ever replace her stock now?"

Justin fingered a pile of glossy green and red peppers. "What about her insurance? That should pay to restock her store."

"Her what?" Mr. Nguyen's knife stopped in midchop. He and Danny both stared at Justin.

"Well, I figured she'd have insurance," Justin said lamely. "I thought all businesses had it."

"In-su-rance?" Mr. Nguyen sounded out the unfamiliar word. "What strange American thing is this?"

Justin looked across at Jenny. Perching on a stool near the old man, she explained, "Insurance is what protects your car or your house against anything bad that happens. You pay the insurance company, and they take care of your house or business if it gets robbed or burned or something."

"You say I must pay this in-su-rance to protect my restaurant?" Mr. Nguyen's dark eyes were suspicious. "So how is this different from the Dragon Tong? They, too, make us pay for protection."

"You pay just a little to the insurance company," Justin explained. "Then if something happens, they give you money to rebuild." He told what he knew about how his parents' insurance policies worked.

When he was finished, Mr. Nguyen shook his head slowly. "This in-su-rance would pay to fix Mrs. Trinh's store?"

"Sure, if she had an insurance policy." Justin's freckled face lit up with sudden excitement. "Don't you see! If the businesses here all had insurance, you wouldn't have to be so afraid of the Dragon Tong. The next time they asked for money, you could just call in the police. If the Dragon Tong got mad and destroyed your business, the insurance company would pay to rebuild it all. The police would round up the Dragon Tong, and you'd be rid of them for good!"

Mr. Nguyen threw him a scornful look as he dropped the diced meat into a large, metal bowl. "Do you think that it is only property that can be destroyed? My family once stood up against evil men. You know what happened. And I know the ways of the police. What can we offer them that they should help us against the powerful hand of the Dragon Tong?"

"But this is America!" Justin argued. "The police here don't work like that. Fighting against criminals is their job. And they help everyone—whether they are rich or poor."

"We've got a friend who is a police officer," Jenny offered. She passed the bowl of meat to Danny who set it beside the stir-fry griddle. "He's great! He'd be glad to help you. If we could convince everyone to stand up together against the Dragon Tong . . ."

"The Vietnamese of this neighborhood are only peasants!" Mr. Nguyen interrupted sharply. "They will not stand up to fight."

Justin stood beside the old man. "But what about you?" he pleaded. "They'd listen to you! If you all got together . . ."

"Maybe he's right, *Ông Nội!*" Danny straightened up. Justin glanced at him with surprise. He hadn't expected his friend to support him. But Danny stared at his grandfather as though he'd been presented with a new idea.

"You know everyone around here respects you, *Ông Nôi*. After all, you're a teacher! Your family was well known in Vietnam. I'll bet they *would* listen to you."

"No! I am too old to stand against the Dragon Tong. And I will not risk the life of my grandson. Have I not lost enough?"

"But, *Ông Nôi!*" Danny protested.

"We have wasted enough time in talk." Mr. Nguyen made a shooing motion, then reached for a mound of shrimp. "I have a restaurant to run. Danny, why do you not take your friends outside?"

Giving them a meaningful glance, Danny jerked his head toward the kitchen door. He looked as rebellious as Justin felt. Once they were out in the dining area, he said in a low voice, "Look, guys. I've got to talk to you."

He stopped. The front door swung open, and Hue walked into the restaurant. He paid no attention to the three teenagers, but strode toward a cupboard at the back of the room and began shaking out clean tablecloths.

"Come on. We can talk upstairs." Danny led the way upstairs at an angry pace. He slammed the living room door behind them and burst out, "You guys are right, and *Ông Nôi* is wrong! I don't want to spend the rest of my life running from the Dragon Tong—or giving them everything we've got!"

Lowering his voice, he added fiercely, "You heard what my grandfather said. My parents died rather than give in to the Vietcong. And look at us! If they're really up in that heaven you talk about, they must be pretty ashamed of us—letting those creeps push us around like this! I mean, am I a total wimp or what?"

Justin couldn't help grinning at Danny who stood feet apart, elbows thrust out, his round jaw clenched with determination. Then he remembered how his friend had faced down three bullies twice his size. "You're no coward, Danny," he said soberly.

"Well, I've made up my mind!" Danny's eyes narrowed under the flopping, black bangs. "It's time we did something about the Dragon Tong."

Relaxing his stance, he looked eagerly at his friends. "So, where do we start?"

Justin was completely taken aback. "Well . . . uh . . . ," he stammered. "What I said about the Dragon Tong . . . I didn't mean . . . I mean, we can't—"

He collected his thoughts. "Look, Danny you got after me for running out there this afternoon. And you were right—it was stupid. Catching the Dragon Tong is a job for the police."

"Yeah, what can the three of us do?" Jenny jumped in just as Danny opened his mouth to protest. "I mean, the police don't even believe us. Besides, those Dragon Tong men are dangerous!"

Danny's face fell, but he said defiantly, "I don't care! You were the ones who said the Dragon Tong should be stopped. If I have to, I'll go after them alone!"

Jenny's voice softened. "Look, Danny, I wish there *was* something we could do to help."

"Maybe there *is* something we can do!" The statement fell like a stone into the argument. Danny and Jenny turned to stare at Justin.

Justin had been preoccupied ever since his encounter with the

Dragon Tong member. Now he ran his fingers through his rusty curls as he always did when he was thinking hard. "I've been thinking, Danny. Why is everyone so scared of the Dragon Tong?"

When Danny gave him an astonished look, Justin added quickly, "It's because they show up in those martial arts suits, right? They look scary and do mean things. And since nobody knows who's behind those masks, they're all afraid to say anything for fear that the Dragon Tong will show up and wreck their businesses."

"So?" Danny tapped his foot.

"So what if you knew who that guy behind the mask was? What if he was just your next-door neighbor or something?" Justin knit his reddish-brown eyebrows together as he thought aloud. "You wouldn't be so ready to hand over your money, right? Maybe you'd even want to get back at him."

"I guess that depends on how big and mean your next-door neighbor is," Danny said dryly. "But I see what you're getting at."

"So what if we found out exactly who these guys are?" Justin's green eyes glowed with excitement. "We could tell your grandfather and the other businesspeople. I mean, if they actually knew who was stealing their money they'd want to stop them, wouldn't they? I'll bet they'd be glad to help the police catch them!"

"Maybe," Danny admitted. "But how are we supposed to do that? No one ever sees their faces."

"I was just getting to that. I know who one of them is."

"What do you mean?" Danny demanded with disbelief. "How can you know?"

Justin didn't answer. Instead, he asked, "Look, Danny, how much do you know about this Hue guy? How long has he worked here?"

Danny shrugged. "I don't know! He came with the restaurant. When my grandfather bought the place about a year ago, he stayed on. Like I told you, he's some distant cousin. Why?"

Now it was Justin's turn to shrug. "Well, you know that Dragon Tong guy out there? The one that came back? I especially noticed him because he was built big like Hue. *And* like the guy who took your grandfather's money the other night."

"So? You think Hue's the only Vietnamese with a decent build in the neighborhood?"

"That's not all." Ignoring Danny's sarcastic interruption, Justin went on, "When he walked over toward me out there . . ." Justin paused until he was sure he had the others' complete attention, then he lowered his voice to a mysterious whisper. "His left eye twitched, twice!"

"His left eye . . ." Danny stiffened. "Hue! His left eye twitches every time he gets mad! Come to think of it, he's never been around when the Dragon Tong showed up to collect! And the way they always know how much money we've made. Hue must be looking through Grandfather's books. If I know where Grandfather keeps the key, I'll bet Hue does too."

"So what do you think your grandfather would do if he found out Hue was one of the Dragon Tong?" Justin asked.

"I'll bet he'd be so mad he'd be glad to call in the police. After the way he's given him a job—and a home! Why that rotten skunk!" Danny sputtered with rage.

"Now wait a minute, guys." Jenny looked from one boy to

the other. "Justin, you can't know for sure that guy out there was Hue. You can't go around accusing people without proof."

"Sure it's Hue!" Danny brushed aside her objection. "I never did like that guy." He started for the door. "And what's more, I know how we can prove it. Come on!"

Danny led them upstairs and stopped at the last door on the right. "This is Hue's room. He always keeps it locked." He pulled a key from his pocket with a dramatic flourish. "But Hue isn't the only one who can play around with locks. I found a master key for the whole building downstairs when we moved in."

Justin kept a cautious lookout as Danny inserted the key into the lock. Once they were inside, he cast one last glance down the empty hall and pulled the door shut.

Hue's bedroom was small and sparsely furnished. A camp cot spread with a blanket stood against the far wall. The only other furniture was a battered dresser and an old chest. Lifting the lid of the chest, Danny rummaged inside.

"So, what are we looking for?" Jenny looked around the bare walls of the room with distaste.

"Shh! Not so loud!" Danny turned around, closing the chest lid quietly. Moving over to the dresser, he whispered, "If Hue's in the Dragon Tong, he's got to have one of those costumes. And this is the only place in the restaurant he could hide it."

While Danny searched the dresser, Justin and Jenny checked under the thin mattress of the cot and in the small closet in one corner.

Danny's shoulders sagged as he closed the last drawer. "Well, if Hue *is* a member of the Dragon Tong, he's too smart to keep anything in here."

"It was him," Justin insisted. "But I don't know how we can prove it."

"Maybe we'll just have to tail him." Jenny wiped her dusty hands on her jeans. "Like the police do."

"Tail him." Danny looked thoughtful. Then his voice rose. "That's it!"

He lowered his voice to an excited whisper. "The Dragon Tong always comes the last weekend of the month to collect the money. That's this weekend! Why don't you spend the night? All we'd have to do is wait until the guy shows and follow him."

"Hey, I was just kidding!" Jenny protested.

"No, that's a great idea!" Justin silently closed the closet door, then checked to make sure they'd left everything as they'd found it. "If it really is Hue, we can find out where he's going and maybe find out who the other members of the Dragon Tong are, too. Between the three of us, we should be able to keep an eye on him."

"I promised I wouldn't call the police. But if we can identify the members of the Dragon Tong, I'm sure Ông Nôi will call the police himself. And if he won't . . ." Danny stopped.

"Then we will!" Justin finished. "We never promised not to call the police."

Jenny didn't look too enthusiastic. "And what if Hue catches us tailing him?"

"Oh, I'm not afraid of Hue!" Danny locked the door and slipped the key into his pocket. "That lazy bum is too much of a coward to hurt anyone."

"No?" The soft, guttural syllable came from behind them.

Chapter Eight

TEEN DETECTIVES

The three teenagers whirled around. Hue lounged against a wall, his broad features expressionless. The hairs on the back of Justin's neck tingled as the restaurant assistant's cool gaze traveled from Danny to the twins.

"I . . . I was just showing Justin and Jenny the house." Moving away from the door, Danny made a frantic motion for them to follow. Hue's mouth curved in a sardonic smile as they edged past him, but he made no attempt to stop them.

"If that guy doesn't stop sneaking up like that . . . ," Jenny said breathlessly as they clattered downstairs.

Justin elbowed Danny in the ribs, teasing him slyly, "I thought you weren't afraid of Hue!"

"I'm not!" Danny repeated scornfully, but he kept his voice low as he glanced back up the stairs. "I was . . . just startled."

He skidded to a stop as they reached the bottom of the stairs. "Look, guys! You don't have to do this, you know. I mean, there's no reason *you* should stick your necks out on this."

"No reason!" Justin snorted. "You're our friend, aren't you? As if we'd let you face that Dragon Tong guy alone! Besides, if you're right about Hue, there's not much danger anyway."

He looked over at Jenny. She still didn't look enthusiastic, but she nodded. Justin turned back to Danny. "It's settled, then. We'll be here Friday afternoon. You're sure the Dragon Tong will show up then?"

Danny shrugged. "Sometimes they come Friday—sometimes Saturday. But they always come the last weekend of the month."

Rattling dishes and the roar of supper customers greeted the three teenagers as they entered the dining area. Danny glanced around the crowded restaurant. "I'd better go help my grandfather, seeing as Hue is upstairs resting. I'll see you at school."

He took one step toward the kitchen, then stopped and turned around. "Hey, Justin . . . you know what *Ông Nôi* said about my parents and all?"

Justin was taken by surprise. So much had happened that afternoon that he'd forgotten their reason for coming! "Yeah? What about it?"

"Well, it sounds like that Christian stuff was pretty important to them, right?" Danny hunched his shoulders. "So I'd kind of like to know what they believed . . . *if Ông Nôi* changes his mind."

"That's great!" Justin exclaimed, and Jenny added, "We'll just have to pray he does change his mind."

They were bubbling over when they arrived home. Over Mom's barbecued beef ribs, they poured out Mr. Nguyen's story and all that had happened that afternoon. But when Jenny started in on their plans to tail Hue, Justin gave her a warning nudge. Danny thought Hue was harmless, but his parents might not see it that way.

"You sure have a knack for stumbling into trouble," Dad joked when they were finished. "Just be careful, will you?"

After supper Justin and Jenny spread out a jigsaw puzzle on the coffee table while Dad relaxed in his easy chair. Jenny suddenly asked, "Dad, why do you think God let the Vietcong shoot Danny's parents?"

Justin glanced up. "Yeah, Dad! I've been wondering the same thing. I mean, they were telling people about Jesus."

Dad had his nose buried in a computer magazine, but after a moment, he looked up. "Do you know what a martyr is?"

Jenny frowned. "Isn't that someone who dies for what he believes?"

"Like Danny's parents," Justin added. "They were killed for telling people about Jesus."

"That's right. Danny's parents were martyrs." Laying down his magazine, Dad looked from one sober face to the other. "God never promised to give Christians an easy life. There have been countless Christians over the centuries who have suffered and even died for their faith in God—starting clear back with Jesus' own disciples. Right now there are thousands of Christians in many countries facing danger because they love Jesus."

Leaning back in his easy chair and lacing his fingers behind his head, Dad went on, "A lot of people think that if they love God, nothing bad will ever happen to them. But Jesus Christ Himself gave up His own life for us, and He told His disciples that they too would face suffering and hardship for His sake. No, kids, God never promised to give us an easy time. But He does promise to be with us and help us in the hard times. And God promises to make even the bad things that happen to us turn out for the best in the end—even if we don't understand it at the time."

"Like the Bible verse we learned at camp," Jenny said thoughtfully. "Romans 8:28."

Dad leaned over to pick up a puzzle piece. "It's kind of like this puzzle. You take this piece now. Anyone looking at it would say it serves no purpose at all, but when you put it here . . ." He snapped the piece into an opening they hadn't noticed. ". . . it finishes a mountain range! We only see our own little puzzle piece. God sees the whole picture!"

Justin knit his eyebrows together. "So what good was there in Danny's parents getting shot by the Vietcong?"

Dad sat back. "Think about it."

Wednesday was Mom's birthday. She acted surprised when she saw her new office. Then, to Justin and Jenny's delight, Dad drove the family to the La Vie Restaurant where they introduced their parents to Mr. Nguyen.

They had just finished their meal when Mr. Nguyen approached the table. Bowing, he asked to speak with Dad. Justin and Jenny gave each other a puzzled look as the two men left the room. They were gone for a half hour.

"I'll take care of it first thing tomorrow," Dad said when they finally reappeared.

Mr. Nguyen waved aside Dad's attempts to pay for their meal. Justin and Jenny waited only until they had piled into the SUV before they burst out, "So what did he want, Dad?"

Dad's hazel eyes twinkled at their open curiosity. "Mr. Nguyen asked to consult with me about some business matters."

🐉

"Hue's here right now!" Danny told Justin and Jenny as they carried their sleeping bags and backpacks upstairs for the weekend. "Let's go see what he's up to."

The twins and Danny slipped quietly downstairs just in time to see Hue walk into the kitchen.

"He's going outside," Danny said breathlessly, peering around the swinging door. Mr. Nguyen raised a surprised eyebrow as the three teenagers pushed by him, mumbling a hurried greeting.

"Look! He's leaving!" Justin whispered triumphantly, catching sight of Hue striding across the empty lot. "And he's carrying something."

"Yeah, the garbage," Jenny retorted. Sure enough, the restaurant assistant was carrying a heavy plastic bag in each hand. He dropped the bags into a corner dumpster. Danny and the twins ducked back into the kitchen as he started back.

The three teenagers tried to stay out of sight as they trailed Hue that afternoon. But the restaurant was not a big place, and time and again they peeked around a corner only to meet Hue's scowling stare. By supper hour, they'd seen nothing out of the ordinary and had only annoyed Danny's grandfather as well as Hue.

"Do such good students not have homework to do?" Mr. Nguyen demanded impatiently, glancing up from his pots to catch them peering stealthily around the back door. "Cops and robbers is a game for children."

"This is ridiculous!" Jenny said, after Hue caught them lurking in the hallway again. "We're just making him suspicious."

Danny's face fell. "But we don't want him to get away!"

Justin snapped his fingers. "I've got it!"

He turned to Danny. "Look, when this Dragon Tong guy comes, your grandfather has to pay him, right?"

Danny nodded a puzzled agreement.

"So instead of following Hue," Justin finished, "how about we follow Mr. Nguyen?"

"Hey, that's a good idea!" Danny exclaimed. He started toward the stairs. "Come on, you two. Let's go help with supper."

If Mr. Nguyen was surprised by the three teenagers' sudden offer to help, he didn't say so but waved them toward a mountainous pile of dirty pots and pans. Danny and the twins began reluctantly to scrub. But even though they worked until the restaurant closed for the night, they saw no sign of a mysterious black figure. And every time Justin poked his head out the kitchen door, he saw Hue hard at work waiting on tables.

"Maybe they've decided to skip this month," he said gloomily as they trudged upstairs.

Danny shook his head. "They'll come. We'll just have to try again tomorrow."

Justin and Jenny exchanged unenthusiastic glances, but they were up as early as Danny the next morning. Justin was scrubbing pots, and Jenny had just lifted the last tray of flaky pastries from the oven when Danny slipped into the kitchen. "He's here!" he whispered.

Mr. Nguyen pulled off his apron, muttered in Vietnamese, then shuffled toward the door.

"He says to keep out of the way," Danny whispered. He jerked his head toward the back door. "So let's do it!"

Hurrying out the back to the side of the building, they crouched behind some bushes to watch the front door. "That's the way he went last time." Justin pointed out the alley where he'd seen the Dragon Tong member disappear a few days before.

Suddenly they were alerted by the bell of the front door. A black figure with a red-and-gold dragon on his back glided into the street. The man in black walked quickly into the alley. Springing to their feet, the teenagers followed cautiously.

This time they stayed well behind the rapidly moving figure, waiting until the dragon disappeared around a corner before sprinting to catch up. They soon left Danny's neighborhood behind and moved through one of the oldest sections of the city. There was little traffic here, and the brick buildings looked abandoned.

Several times they completely lost sight of the man. But frantic peering around corners always brought a glimpse of the black shadow a block or two away.

Once or twice, Justin had the eerie feeling that they themselves were being followed. But when he looked back, there was no one in sight. *You're losing your mind, Justin!* he told himself sternly after he'd stopped for the third time. He ran to catch up to the other two.

They had stopped at the entrance of a narrow alley that ran between two long, brick buildings.

Justin looked past them. There was no sign of the masked man, and the alley dead-ended in a high concrete wall. "Where did he go?" Then he spotted a narrow door halfway down the alley to their right.

Jenny nodded toward the door. "He's got to be in there. He didn't have time to climb that wall."

Tiptoeing down the alley, they stopped outside the metal door. Justin tried the handle. It was unlocked. Easing the door open a few inches, he listened breathlessly for any movement inside. But he heard only the heavy pounding of his own heart, and after a moment, he opened the door wider and slipped inside, Jenny and Danny pressing on his heels.

The inside seemed dark after the outdoors. As his eyes adjusted to the gloom, Justin saw that they were in some sort of warehouse. Empty barrels and crates and piles of scrap lumber and metal littered the huge room, but it was obvious that the building had not been occupied for some time. The air was heavy with mildew, and years of dust lay everywhere.

Easing the door shut behind them, they edged sideways away from the door. The plastered wall felt cold under Justin's hands, and he was nervously aware of their exposed position. He saw no sign of the man they'd been following, but across the vast floor along the far wall he could make out several doors. What looked like a supervisor's office jutted out into one corner of the warehouse, its long window overlooking the storage area. Motioning for Danny and Jenny to follow him, Justin crept across the floor to a stack of crates that towered over his head.

Once they were safely out of sight, he whispered, "So what do you want to do now, Danny? That guy could be long gone."

"Hey, guys! Over here!" Jenny said softly. She slid over to the far end of the stack of crates and stared hard into the shadows. The two boys scrambled over beside her. Then they saw it too— a flicker of motion behind the long office window.

Danny grabbed Justin's arm hard. "That's got to be him. Come on!"

This time it was Danny and Jenny who took the lead, sneaking from the crates to a pile of barrels, then making a dash to crouch behind a mound of old scaffolding, so quickly and silently that Justin could hardly keep up. He smothered a cry of pain as he stubbed his toe against a stray two-by-four. If he could just get his own big feet to move as silently as the other two!

There was something spooky about the huge, dark room. A faint rustle somewhere behind him made him start, and he glanced back uneasily half-expecting to feel a hard hand come down on his shoulder. But he saw only shadows, and it wasn't long before they were crouched under the long window of the foreman's office. Justin raised his head to peek over the sill. He drew in a sharp breath as he saw what was inside!

A circle of black figures stood around a long wooden table. The backs of those nearest to the window flamed with the serpent dragon of the Dragon Tong.

Justin counted the black figures. Six! The same number he'd seen outside Mrs. Trinh's grocery. This must be the entire gang!

The Dragon Tong members were all masked, but he easily picked out the man they had followed from the restaurant. He was a full head taller than the others. As Justin watched, the big Vietnamese pulled a stack of bills from his black costume and tossed it on the table.

"That's our money!" Danny whispered savagely in Justin's ear.

The others added their own stacks of money to the table. The biggest of the Dragon Tong snapped a phrase in Vietnamese.

Across the table, one of the masked figures pushed back his black hood and pulled the coverings from his mouth.

"Hey, that's Kiet Lam from the pawnshop!" Danny whispered as a thin face emerged.

One by one, the members of the Dragon Tong slid back their hoods. The big man they had followed was the last to remove his mask. Justin watched in breathless anticipation as the black hood slid back to show Hue's broad, dark features. He'd been right! He flashed the other two a triumphant grin as the restaurant worker began to talk in low, rapid Vietnamese. Now all they had to do was get out of here and report back to Danny's grandfather.

But Danny didn't return his grin. He was staring at Hue as though he were some stranger he had never seen before. In spite of the shadows that cloaked their hiding place, Justin easily read the fear and dismay on the other boy's face. "What is it, Danny?" he whispered. "What's he saying?"

"I can't believe this!" Danny's whisper was taut with anger and horror. "Hue isn't just a *member* of the Dragon Tong, he's their leader!"

"Their leader!" Justin was neither as surprised nor as horrified as Danny. He raised his eyes again over the edge of the window. Hue's hands were gesturing rapidly, and his low, harsh tones sounded as though he were snapping out orders. "So what's he saying? And who are the others?"

But Danny's only answer was a muffled grunt. And when Justin glanced sideways, he saw a black hand clapped over the mouth of his friend!

Chapter Nine

NO WAY OUT

Justin's horrified gaze traveled up the shadowed outline that hauled Danny to his feet. A second shadow reached black fingers for Jenny. Justin opened his mouth to warn her, but nothing came out. For a moment he crouched frozen, staring up at the two masked figures.

"Justin, run!"

Jenny's urgent cry broke off as her captor clapped a hand over her mouth. Leaping to his feet, Justin whirled to see Hue's startled glare through the glass window of the office. The Dragon Tong leader shouted an order in Vietnamese. Justin dashed across the warehouse.

Behind him, the sound of harsh yells and running feet erupted into the warehouse. Justin dove for cover behind a pair of old steel drums. *How could you have been so stupid?* he demanded of himself.

It was easy now to guess what had happened. That eerie sensation of someone following them hadn't been his imagination after all. Other Dragon Tong members hurrying to the meeting must have seen the three teenagers trailing their leader and followed them in turn. *And just because I counted only six of them at Mrs. Trinh's grocery, I assumed that those men around the table were all of them. I didn't even bother keeping a lookout! Some detective I make!*

The members of the Dragon Tong fanned out through the warehouse, running swiftly to block his escape. Crouched low behind the pile of boxes, Justin scanned the huge storage area. But it took only a moment to realize that his only way out was through the narrow side door through which they had entered.

I've got to reach that door! Justin threaded his way across the warehouse, dodging from one pile of debris to another.

But he had covered only half the distance when he saw Hue step out from behind a stack of lumber a few yards to his right. Justin ducked behind a pillar, but not before Hue had caught sight of him. The Dragon Tong leader moved with a long, powerful stride to cut him off. Justin threw a frantic glance around him. There were no other Dragon Tong members closeby. Maybe— just maybe—he could still reach that door first!

Stretching his legs in a desperate sprint, Justin headed straight across the vast, open floor and for a few seconds he was sure he was going to make it. But Hue was incredibly swift. A heavy blow between his shoulders knocked Justin to the ground.

"So! You think you can escape from me!" Hue said. Justin scrambled backward. But the Dragon Tong leader pounced, dragging him to his feet. Steel-strong fingers dug into Justin's neck as Hue forced him back across the warehouse to where Danny and Jenny were being guarded.

Justin gave Jenny a questioning look as Hue shoved him over beside them. She nodded that she was okay. Danny looked dazed as he stared with disbelief at the leader of the Dragon Tong.

The other Dragon Tong members formed a loose circle around their captives. Folding his arms across his broad chest, Hue gave the three teenagers a thoughtful look. "So! This is why you follow me around the restaurant. You are putting your tongue in Hue's business!"

Justin's heart was still pounding, but a cold anger burned inside as he glanced from Hue's self-satisfied expression to Danny's stunned face. "*Nose,* you mean!" he retorted.

"What do you mean?" The big Vietnamese gave Justin a suspicious look. "What is this about a nose?"

Justin glared up at Hue, his back stiff with contempt and defiance. "You stick your *nose* in people's business, not your tongue."

"So! You make fun of Hue!" The Dragon Tong leader took a menacing step toward Justin, his broad face dark with anger.

"Justin, are you crazy?" Jenny elbowed Justin sharply in the ribs. "Don't make him mad!"

Justin subsided, but now Danny stepped forward, his stunned expression giving way to bewildered anger as he planted himself aggressively in front of the Dragon Tong leader.

"Hue, how could you do this to us?" he demanded. "After everything *Ông Nôi* has done for you? I mean, he was the one who talked Mr. Kwan into giving you a job. And he kept you on when he bought the restaurant. He gave you a home!"

He glanced around at the silent circle that surrounded them. "All of you! How could you do this to your own people?"

Hue spat contemptuously on the floor. "Your grandfather with his fine restaurant! These neighbors getting rich! What have they done for us?"

"But we're not rich!" Danny protested. "You know how hard *Ông Nôi* worked to buy that restaurant!"

The Dragon Tong leader ignored Danny's interruption. He waved a hand at his followers. "In Vietnam—in the camps, we were feared! People trembled when we passed by. They gave us the best there was!"

"So you were criminals in the refugee camps, too," Danny muttered at the floor. "Are we supposed to cheer?"

"In America, we clean floors and wash dishes," Hue continued as though he hadn't heard Danny's comment, but Justin noticed that his left eyelid was starting to twitch. "In Vietnam I would not touch such work. There I would be an important man!"

Raising his head, Danny stared scornfully around the circle of men. "In Vietnam you'd probably be dead. The Vietcong shoot thieves and street scum!"

Justin guessed that some of the Dragon Tong didn't understand English, but several took a step forward. Justin's mouth went dry as he glanced around at the cold, watchful eyes and hostile expressions. Most of the Dragon Tong weren't much taller than Justin, but their well-trained muscles rippled under the smooth silk, and Justin had no doubt these men were experienced fighters.

"You!" Hue's nostrils flared with fury. Striding forward, he backhanded Danny so hard that his head snapped sideways. "You I have hated most of all! Always telling me to do this, do that! Always bossing!"

Danny staggered backward, one hand to his reddened cheek. "You always were a rotten worker!"

"Enough!" Hue raised his hand again, his broad chest rising

and falling with his anger. Then he dropped his hand to his side and he said, "From now on, it will be you who do as I say!"

Danny's back stiffened with outrage. "We're not afraid of you." But his defiance didn't sound very convincing.

A cruel smile played around Hue's thick lips. Leaning forward, he said softly, "Then you are very foolish."

Justin had heard enough. While he admired Danny's courage, it was only getting them into more trouble. Giving Danny a warning nudge, he said quietly, "Look, Hue! Why don't you let us go before the cops show up."

"Yeah!" Stepping up beside her brother, Jenny brushed her hand against his. Her fingers were ice cold, and Justin knew that she was just as frightened as he. "If you hurt us or . . . kill us, you'll have cops down here no matter what all your neighbors say."

"The cops! Do you think they will listen to you?" The Dragon Tong leader flicked a finger at the black silk that covered his body. "There is nothing illegal here. Other martial arts groups wear such clothes. And no one has ever seen us take money. To the police, the Dragon Tong does not exist."

He paused, then gave a sudden nod. "But you are right. Killing will bring too many police. It will be enough to keep you quiet."

Justin let his shoulders slump with relief, but Danny burst out, "You think we're going to keep quiet? When *Ông Nôi* finds out that you're the one stealing all our money he won't give you another cent!"

He glared around at the other Dragon Tong members. "Nor will anyone else. They'll be glad to talk to the police once they know who you are."

To Justin's astonishment, Hue threw back his head and laughed—a harsh, jeering laugh. Thrusting his broad, dark face close to the three teenagers, he hissed, "Fools! Do you really think the Vietnamese people fear us because they do not know who we are?"

He gave Danny a mocking look. "Do you think your grandfather does not guess that I am one of the Dragon Tong? You tell him to fire me. But he is afraid—afraid of what I may do if he sends me away. And these . . ."

He gestured toward the silent tong members. "Do you think there are not those who guess who each of these are? No! Those who guess what lies behind the mask are only more afraid. They will never speak against the Dragon Tong!

"And you!" Hue turned with pantherlike swiftness and Justin found it suddenly hard to breathe. "You come to our neighborhood with your talk of the police. You think you can overthrow the power of the Dragon Tong. You will learn today that the hand of the Dragon Tong is strong!"

Hue raised a hand. Icy fingers crept up Justin's spine as three of the men in black moved forward. "What do you mean?" he demanded desperately. "What are you going to do?"

"It is time the Vietnamese learn what happens to the man who defies the Dragon Tong." Hue looked down at Danny with cold satisfaction. "And it will be your grandfather and his precious restaurant that pays the price."

"But *Ông Nôi* always pays his money!" Danny shouted as one of the Dragon Tong grabbed him by the arm. "He doesn't even know we followed you."

"That does not matter now." Hue turned to Justin and Jenny.

"You two have tried to stir up the Vietnamese against me—against the Dragon Tong. But you will find that you have done nothing to help your friends. You have brought only worse trouble on them."

The Dragon Tong leader gave a sharp order in Vietnamese, then strode off across the warehouse. Justin swallowed as a knife appeared in the hand of the man nearest him. Baring rotted teeth in an unpleasant grin, the tong member indicated that he was to follow.

"Wait a minute!" Jenny pulled back against the man who was dragging her along. "Where are you taking us? You said you'd let us go!"

Hue glanced back over his shoulder. "I said only that I would keep you quiet," he said brusquely. "But if you do as you are told, you will not be hurt. In here!"

He stopped in front of one of the doors scattered along the near wall of the warehouse. The door was solid metal with an old-fashioned lock. Pushing it open, he motioned for them to enter.

The room obviously had not been opened in a long time. Danny wrinkled his nose with disgust at the dank, musty smell that wafted out. "I'm not going in there!" he scowled. But he took a quick step backward when a knife suddenly appeared in the hand of the man who was guarding him.

Justin choked on the smell of mildew as his own guard pushed him through the doorway. He glanced around. The room was small, and its only light came from a narrow window at ceiling height on the far wall. Like the rest of the warehouse it had been abandoned long ago and any furnishings carried off. But a scattered pile of old wood and broken boxes showed that it too had once been used for storage.

"This will hold you!" Lounging against the door frame, Hue studied the dim, airless room for any possible exit. "I do not think you will find it possible to follow us now."

"Where are you going?" Danny demanded. "You'd better not hurt my grandfather!"

"When will you learn that it is I who give orders here now." Hue's face grew ugly as he took a step toward Danny. Danny cringed, one hand flying to his bruised cheek, but his black eyes still glared defiance. The Dragon Tong leader hissed, "To you—to all the Vietnamese—Hue has been nothing. But no more! Now it is I who am powerful and to be feared. After today the Vietnamese people will know that the hand of the Dragon Tong lies everywhere!"

Hue's harsh voice rose with sudden passion. "And it will not be just the Vietnamese who feel my hand. Soon the Dragon Tong will reach far beyond this neighborhood. One day the whole city will tremble at the whisper of my name!"

The Dragon Tong leader fell silent. There was a mad glitter in the black eyes as Hue gazed over their heads, and Justin realized with a sinking heart that the man wasn't totally sane. Hue moved toward the door.

Jenny took a step after him. "So how long are you going to leave us here? When are you coming back?"

Hue turned his burning gaze back to the three teenagers. "We are finished with this place. We will not be coming back."

Justin was surprised and relieved at his answer. Then he heard Danny's angry protest. "You can't leave us here! How are we going to get out?"

"Shout for help!" Hue started again toward the door. "Perhaps in a day or two someone will hear you. Or perhaps not."

"You know no one will hear us!" Danny shouted at Hue. "And nobody knows we're here! We could starve!"

"Then you will not again interfere in my plans," Hue said indifferently, stepping through the door. "And if the police ask questions, it is only three children foolish enough to play in an empty building."

"No! You can't do this!" Danny rushed forward as the heavy metal door swung shut with a dull thud. But a mocking laugh was Hue's only reply, and Danny's face showed his despair as the key turned with a metallic click in the massive lock.

Chapter Ten

SUPERMAN?

"This is all my fault!" Danny burst out as the echoes of the Dragon Tong leader's mocking laughter died away. He paced a restless turn around the small storage room. "I was sure Hue was too much of a lazy coward to be dangerous. I guess I didn't know him at all."

Jenny sneezed. "But he's got to send someone to let us out," she said. "I mean, he promised he wouldn't hurt us!"

"Oh, he won't hurt us!" Danny answered bitterly. He stopped long enough to give the door a savage kick. "Hue won't do anything that will bring a murder charge against him. Leaving us to starve to death is something else."

"Oh, come on, Danny! We won't starve to death." Justin massaged his aching neck. "All we've got to do is call for help. Sooner or later, someone will let us out."

"That's what you think!" Danny retorted. "I've been in this part of the city before. We could call for months before anyone came."

He kicked again at the metal door. "Besides, we've got to get out of here now—not next week. You heard what they said about *Ông Nôi!*"

Jenny sneezed again violently. "You're not kidding we've got to get out of here!" She rubbed her streaming eyes. "I'm allergic to mildew."

"Sure. But how?" Justin demanded.

He looked around the small room. It was one of the ugliest places he'd ever seen. Dampness had splotched the dingy walls with mildew, and cobwebs hung from the ceiling. The continual rains of the Pacific Northwest had leaked across the ceiling and dripped down the walls in one corner, leaving the plaster cracked and peeling. But the door was solid metal. There wasn't even an air vent.

Jenny yelped as a spider crawled on the sleeve of her thin jacket. Brushing it off with a grimace, she suggested, "What about the window? Maybe one of us could climb up there."

Justin eyed the small window. It was far above their heads, and while several feet long, was less than a foot high. Small panes let in a scant light but were obviously never intended to be opened. He shook his head. "Not even you could fit through that," he told his sister. "Even if we could break the glass."

"Maybe I could." Danny studied the window with sudden hope. "I mean, I'm smaller than Jenny. I might be able to squeeze through one of those panes, if you two could get me up there."

"Well, I guess it's worth a try," Justin agreed. "We'll need something to break that glass."

Rummaging through the garbage on the floor, the three teenagers came up with several chunks of brick and scrap metal. Taking turns, they threw the chunks at the window. But it didn't take them long to realize that the panes in the small window were industrial glass tiles several inches thick.

"This isn't going to work." Dropping his piece of brick to the ground, Justin hopelessly surveyed the still-intact window. The optimism he'd felt when Hue shut them in here was fading.

"Maybe we could pound out the glass." Danny beckoned Justin over to the window. "Here, lift me up there."

Justin situated himself under the window, and the smaller boy vaulted to his shoulders. Stretching as far as he could reach, he hammered on the windowpanes with a heavy length of two-by-four. But even with his efforts, the glass tiles showed little more than a few cracks and chips.

"We're just going to have to try calling for help," Jenny insisted when Danny climbed down. She sneezed again. "Maybe someone will be out there. If they're standing right outside, they might hear us."

"How about if we all scream 'Help!' on the count of three," Justin suggested. "Come on! One, two, three!"

They yelled at the top of their lungs, but only silence answered their call. Again, they yelled, then waited for an answer. Still nothing!

They had been calling for perhaps fifteen minutes, and all three were growing hoarse when Danny said impatiently, "We're not getting anywhere with this. There's no one out there, and there never will be!"

"So what do we do now?" Jenny wheezed. "Anyone else got a great idea?"

Dropping to the floor, she pulled her knees up to her chin. Justin gave her a worried look. She kept sneezing, and her eyes were almost swollen shut. He knew that her allergy to mildew was very real, and she would find it increasingly difficult to breathe if they stayed in this damp place.

He dropped down beside her, rubbing at his aching arms and shoulders. "There's only one thing we can do, and we should have done it a long time ago. We're going to pray and ask God to get us out of here."

Danny, who had perched on an upended box, turned his head sharply at Justin's words. But he made no protest when they bowed their heads, and after a moment, he bowed his head, too.

"Dear God," Justin prayed, "You know we've got to get out of here fast. Jenny's sick, and Danny's grandfather's in a lot of trouble. Please send someone by to let us out."

Jenny prayed next, her words mixed with sneezing and coughing.

When they lifted their heads, Danny looked thoughtful. "*Ông Nôi* says that Buddha of ours is just a statue—that it can't hear us praying. What makes you think your God can hear?"

"We know He can." Jenny found a tissue in her jacket pocket and blew her nose. "He's answered our prayers lots of times, hasn't He, Justin?"

"Yeah?" Danny demanded. "So why didn't He save my parents from the Vietcong? Weren't they praying to your same God?" When the twins exchanged a sudden grin, he gave them a suspicious look. "What's so funny?"

"It's just that we asked my dad that same question just the other day," Justin explained.

"So! What did he say?"

Justin pulled his thin jacket tight as he groped for an answer. Now that he was no longer moving, the chill dampness of the abandoned warehouse seeped into his clothes. Wrapping his arms around his knees, he answered slowly. "Dad said some things I didn't quite understand."

He glanced over at his sister. "But there's one thing Jenny and I have found out the hard way these last few months! God does know what He's doing—even when it doesn't make sense to us! Sometimes He doesn't answer our prayers just the way we want him to. But He always answers them. And what *He* decides to do, even if things look bad at the moment, always turns out even better than what we've asked for!"

"Like Romans 8:28," Jenny added softly. "And we know that in all things God works for the good of those who love him."

"Yeah?" Danny looked skeptical. "So what good was there in my parents getting killed?"

During the last few days, Justin often had found himself thinking about his father's last statement. He knit his eyebrows together. "Well, it brought you and your grandfather to America. And maybe other villagers trusted in God when they saw your parents give their lives for what they believed. Maybe other good things happened that we'll never know about!"

"Oh, yeah?" Danny jumped to his feet. "Well, at the moment, I'm more interested in helping my grandfather—and us. Let's see if your God can make something good out of this mess."

Justin was silent. Then he pushed himself wearily to his feet. "The only thing we can do is start calling again. Maybe someone will come into the building in time to hear us."

"And by that time it'll be too late to stop the Dragon Tong," Danny retorted bitterly. "We've got to get out of this room before Hue does something awful to my grandfather."

Jenny had been resting her aching head on her knees. But now she let out a sudden giggle. "Maybe you should get Justin to knock down the walls!"

"Knock down the walls?" Danny stared from one twin to the other.

Jenny raised her head. "Sure! Didn't you know he's the original Superman?" Danny smiled a little as she described how Justin had knocked a hole in the office wall. Justin's freckled face was beet-red by the time she finished.

"It wasn't like that!" he protested. Then he stopped and looked around at the damp, peeling walls of the small room. "Still, why not?"

As the other two stared in astonishment, Justin rushed over to the far corner of the room where a leak had left the walls stained and crumbling. Picking up a chunk of plaster that had fallen to the floor, he said with growing excitement, "Maybe we *could* break through the wall. Look here! This wall isn't made of brick like the outside walls. It's just plaster all the way through."

Following Justin over to the corner, Jenny and Danny studied with wonder the wall that separated their prison from the next room. Danny dug his fingers into a long, damp crack. "It's crazy, man!" he said. But hope was replacing the despair on his face. "But maybe it's just crazy enough to work!"

"Well, let's get going!" Grabbing an iron bar from the pile of scraps in the room, Justin gouged deeply into the hole that the chunk of fallen plaster had left. Another piece of plaster crumbled away.

Danny hurried to bring his own iron bar, and Jenny pounded at the wall with a piece of scrap metal. The floor at their feet was soon covered with mounds of plaster. Chalklike dust coated the three teenagers from head to foot, and the boys were soon sneezing as much as Jenny. But no one minded as they saw the hole in the wall widen and deepen.

It was a letdown when the iron bars thudded against something solid. Scraping away at the plaster, Justin discovered that they had struck a wooden post. Danny, digging frantically at his end of the hole, found another two-by-four wooden stud only eighteen inches from the first. Slats of wood ran from one stud to the other underneath the plaster. These were spaced only inches apart, and there was no way even the smallest person could crawl between them.

Justin wiped the back of his hand across the plaster dust and sweat that streaked his face. "I'm sorry, guys. I guess it was a pretty dumb idea."

But Jenny was still poking away at the hole in the wall. "Hey, guys!" she exclaimed suddenly. "This wood is rotten! I'll bet we could dig through it."

"What?" Grabbing his iron bar, Justin chiseled at the wooden slats. Jenny was right. The same leak that had stained the paint and eaten away at the plaster had seeped deep into the wall. Over the years, the damp had softened and weakened the wooden underpinning until now the rotten wood splintered away under Justin's determined attack.

"Let's get digging!" Justin ordered his two companions. "If we can break through, we can still get out of here."

Forgetting their exhaustion, they renewed their efforts with fresh eagerness. Then something gave way under Justin's bar. He fell hard against the wall as the bar buried itself in the wall clear up to his knuckles.

Recovering his balance, Justin pulled the iron bar slowly out of the wall. Then all three caught their breath with excitement. A pale light was glimmering through a hole the size of a silver dollar!

Chapter Eleven

REVENGE

"Justin, you're a genius!" Throwing her arms around her brother, Jenny hugged him, then hugged a startled Danny. "Come on, guys. Let's get out of here!"

"Hey, calm down!" Justin grinned. "We're not out yet." But it didn't take them long to knock out the remaining plaster, leaving an opening just wide enough to squeeze through. Justin was the first through the hole. He was dismayed to find himself in another storeroom much like the one he had just left, but he soon discovered that this door was unlocked. Moments later, all three were running through the dim, silent warehouse.

"We've got to find my grandfather," Danny said anxiously as they emerged into the alley. "I just hope we're not too late!"

Justin glanced at his watch. It had taken them a good two hours to break free from the storeroom, and it was now well past noon. Even if Hue had stopped to make plans, the Dragon Tong must have reached the restaurant long ago.

"We'd better call Lieutenant Adams first." Jenny shook the white plaster dust from her hair and clothes. She was already breathing easier in the crisp breeze of the September afternoon. "I don't feel like taking on the Dragon Tong alone again."

Danny opened his mouth to protest, but Justin cut in, "Jenny's right. If the Dragon Tong has your grandfather, we're going to need help. It's time we called in the police!"

Danny hesitated, then nodded a reluctant agreement. "Okay. We'll look for a pay phone on the way. Now let's go!"

The last hour had been an exhausting one, but Danny set the pace at a fast trot. He slowed down only when they approached a telephone booth near the restaurant.

"Make it fast!" Danny snapped.

Justin lifted the receiver and punched "0" for the operator. A female voice said, "This is the operator, how may I help you?"

"Get me the police!" Justin gasped out, still out of breath. "This is an emergency!"

Danny thrust his head in the telephone booth impatiently. Justin shook his head, then turned back to the phone as a new voice came on the line. "Seattle Police Department . . ."

Justin broke in. "May I speak to Lieutenant Adams? Tell him it's Justin Parker. It's an emergency!"

Danny thrust his head back into the telephone booth. "What's taking so long?"

Justin grimaced, gesturing at the receiver in his hand. "They've put me on hold again!"

"Well, I can't wait any longer!" Danny said sharply. "I've got to find *Ông Nôi!*" He jerked his thumb toward the glass side of the telephone booth, his round face angry and worried. "The restaurant's just two blocks down that way. You guys stay here and wait for that cop friend of yours."

"No! Danny, wait!" But he had already ducked out of the

booth, and a voice in Justin's ear called his attention back to the phone.

"Hello, Justin!" It was a man's voice this time, crisp and authoritative. "Lieutenant Adams is out right now. Can I give him a message for you?"

"No, I've got to talk to Lieutenant Adams! No one else will believe me!" Justin glanced up as a sharp tapping sounded on the glass door. Jenny motioned frantically toward Danny already a block away and running full speed. Justin nodded, then said urgently into the phone, "Please, you've got to get me through to him. It's a matter of life and death! Someone might get killed if you don't hurry!"

"I'm sorry, kid. If you'll leave a message, I'll get it to him as soon as I can."

Justin's shoulders slumped. "Please tell Lieutenant Adams to get down to La Vie Restaurant right away. He'll know where it is. The Dragon Tong are going after Danny Nguyen's grandfather."

"The Dragon Tong?" The police officer on the other end sounded suspicious. "This isn't some kind of prank, is it?"

"This is for real!" Justin said. "Lieutenant Adams'll understand! Just tell him it's Justin Parker calling."

"What took so long?" Jenny demanded, as he stepped out of the booth.

"I couldn't get Lieutenant Adams," Justin told her. "But I left a message. They said they'd get it to him right away."

"Well, I hope he comes pretty soon!" Jenny tried to stifle another sneeze, but failed. Her puffy brown eyes were dark with worry. "If Hue's got Mr. Nguyen, there's no telling what Danny'll do."

"Yeah, I know," Justin said gloomily. "We'd better go find him."

They broke into a run, stopping behind the restaurant. A gravel alley separated the restaurant from the next building.

Justin scanned the parking area that ran from the restaurant back to the street. Apart from a couple of parked cars, it was empty. He looked down the alley. It too was empty except for a large, metal recycling bin. Justin swallowed his disappointment. He hadn't really expected to find Danny waiting for them. But how were they to go about finding him?

"I sure don't see Danny," Jenny echoed his thoughts. "Or the Dragon Tong."

"If the Dragon Tong are here, they're probably inside or out front," Justin said. "And if they're not . . ." He paused, and Jenny finished, "Then all we've got to do is find Danny and his grandfather and clear out of here until the police show up."

She added sarcastically, "Let's just check it out first before we go barging in this time!" She jerked her head toward the recycling bin at the end of the alley. "We should be able to see from there."

Justin scanned the area again to make sure no one was in sight, then followed his sister down the alley. Reaching the recycling bin, they squeezed between it and the wall.

From their position behind the bin, they had a clear view not only of the restaurant but of the street that ran in front of it. The metal top of the bin stood open, and the narrow space between the hinged lid and the side of the bin allowed them to look out without being seen. Lunchtime on a Saturday was not a popular shopping time, but the small sprinkling of Asian shoppers strolling down the street or peeking into store windows seemed perfectly normal. There was no sign of the Dragon Tong.

"It doesn't look like they've done anything to the restaurant," Jenny whispered hopefully. "Maybe Hue changed his mind. Maybe they're not coming!"

"He probably got scared and decided to clear out of town," Justin whispered back. He straightened up as though a load of bricks had fallen off his shoulders. "Let's go see if we can just find Danny and Mr. Nguyen."

He'd hardly finished speaking when he heard the faint crunch of soft footsteps in gravel. Squatting down, Justin watched as a black figure rounded the back corner of the restaurant. "The Dragon Tong!" he said. "They showed up after all!"

The man in the silk mask walked slowly along the near side of the restaurant. In one hand he carried a red, five-gallon container just like the ones Dad used for extra gasoline on camping trips. At each of the first-story windows, he paused to splash a clear liquid against the wooden frame.

"Hey, that's gas!" Justin exclaimed as a sickly odor reached him across the alley. He slapped a hand to his forehead. "So that's how Hue plans to show 'the power of the Dragon Tong'. They're going to torch the restaurant!"

"What do you mean—burn it?" Jenny peered out at the three-story building. "But it's brick!"

"Everything inside is made of wood, isn't it?" Justin waited impatiently until the Dragon Tong member had retraced his steps to the back of the building, then jumped to his feet. "Come on! We've got to warn Danny before he gets caught inside."

"I'm afraid he already knows." Jenny yanked her brother back down behind the cover of the recycling bin. "Look!"

A small group of Vietnamese had just emerged from the front

door of the restaurant. Behind them, herding them along, were a full half dozen of the Dragon Tong. Justin groaned as he caught sight of a small, struggling captive. It was Danny!

The street in front of the restaurant emptied quickly as the Dragon Tong members fanned out across the pavement. The Vietnamese customers who had been eating lunch in La Vie Restaurant scurried to take shelter inside the other stores. Within seconds, there was no one left in the street but the Dragon Tong. But Justin saw a pair of dark eyes peering from the jewelry shop window, and he knew that many others were watching from a safe distance.

A great audience for Hue's revenge! he thought bitterly.

The Vietnamese boy was kicking and struggling wildly against his captor. The Dragon Tong members all wore their hoods again, but Justin knew by his size that the black figure that held Danny pinned against him with one powerful arm was Hue.

"You can't burn the place!" Danny shouted. "*Ông Nôi* is in there!"

Justin and Jenny exchanged a worried glance. "They wouldn't burn the place with someone in it, would they?" Jenny whispered.

"No, of course not!" Justin reassured her, but his freckled face was troubled. He threw a quick glance up and down the street. This would be a perfect moment for the police to show up. *Come on, Lieutenant Adams! Where are you?*

Hue shifted his grip to the scruff of Danny's neck. His hood was still drawn tight over his forehead, but he had pulled down the strip of silk that masked his mouth, and Justin saw that he was laughing as he held Danny at arm's length a few inches off the pavement.

The Dragon Tong leader spoke. Justin couldn't make out what he was saying, but Danny's voice rose angrily. "I don't know where they are, and I don't care! Where's my grandfather?"

Hue growled an answer. Danny's voice rose again. "I don't believe you! If he's not inside, then where is he?"

Twisting suddenly in Hue's grip, he sank his teeth through the black silk into the Dragon Tong leader's arm. With a yelp of pain, Hue shook Danny loose, knocking him to the pavement. Danny scrambled backward, but Hue reached him easily before he could escape.

The Dragon Tong leader was no longer laughing. Yanking Danny to his feet, he punched him hard across the face. Still holding Danny in the air, he reached with his other hand into a hidden pocket. Justin's eyes widened as Hue pulled out a box of long, camping matches. With a quick order, he tossed them to one of his men.

"Please!" Danny struggled harder than ever. "You've got to get Ông Nôi out! You can't leave him in there!"

His pleading was directed to the Dragon Tong leader. But as his voice rose, Danny turned his head to glance across the street, his black eyes shooting a desperate appeal for help, right to the spot where Justin and Jenny crouched hidden behind the recycling bin!

Chapter Twelve

FIERY PERIL

"Danny saw us!" Justin whispered with astonishment as Hue shoved Danny toward another of his men. "We've got to help!"

Justin didn't know how, but he had no doubt that the Vietnamese boy's appeal for help had been aimed at them. He stood up, carefully hiding behind the dumpster. "We've got to get Mr. Nguyen out."

"Are you crazy?" Jenny gasped. "They're about to burn the place down! Besides, we don't even know if Mr. Nguyen is in there!"

"It'll only take a minute to check." Justin's freckled face was set hard with determination. "Look, Jenny, I'm scared too, but we're the only help Danny's got. Anyway, he wouldn't be in this mess if we hadn't encouraged him to stand up against the Dragon Tong."

Jenny got to her feet with a sigh. "So what do we do now?"

Justin glanced across the street. The Dragon Tong member with the matches argued and gestured toward the building. Justin suddenly realized that only six of the eight Dragon Tong members stood out on the street.

"They can't torch the place yet," he whispered. "There's still someone inside!"

Justin looked across the alley. He glanced back at the Dragon

Tong. Hue snatched the matches impatiently from his follower's hand. No one was looking in their direction.

"Let's go!" Grabbing Jenny's hand, Justin dashed across the alley. They dove behind one of the parked cars, then crouched along the brick wall. When they reached the back corner of the restaurant, Justin thrust a cautious head around the corner. To his relief, the Dragon Tong had not posted a guard.

"Man, I wish the cops were here!" he muttered, as they slipped around the corner. He turned suddenly to his sister. "Jenny, why don't you go back to that pay phone. We're going to need the police even if we do get Mr. Nguyen out."

"No way! I'm not leaving you here!" Jenny protested. "What if you get trapped inside?"

"I can be in and out of there in two minutes," Justin insisted. "But we've got to hurry!"

He gave her a little push. Still reluctant, she hurried across the back parking lot. Justin moved quickly along the back wall. Cracking open the kitchen door, he listened for any sound inside. He heard nothing, but he hesitated, his heart racing. Did he really want to do this?

Taking a deep breath, Justin pushed the door open and slipped inside. The kitchen smelled of spilled gasoline. The soft tinkle of a bell drew his attention to the swinging door, just in time to see the front door slam behind a black figure with a red-and-gold dragon flaming from his back.

That's it! They're out! Fear quickened Justin's footsteps as he checked the big dining area and pantry, then bounded up the stairs. He knew he had only minutes—perhaps seconds—before a tossed match could send the whole building up in flames.

Justin glanced around the living room. There was no sign of Mr. Nguyen. He started down the hall quickly. The doors all stood open—so the fire would spread faster, he guessed. At least it made his job easier! He glanced into one empty room after another. A shock wave ran through him when he heard footsteps ahead. Diving into the storeroom he peered through a crack. A door opened at the end of the hall, and a short, masked figure stepped out. Behind him, Justin caught a glimpse of narrow, wooden stairs climbing upward.

Of course! Justin groaned inwardly. *This is a three-story building!*

He'd never been past the Nguyen's living quarters, and he hadn't even known there was a stairway beyond that door.

The Dragon Tong member carried a red gas can. He paused to splash its contents up the stairs, then hurried down the corridor. Justin eased back into the hall as the man disappeared down the stairwell. At least they couldn't start the fire until he got out! Casting a hasty glance into the last storeroom, he hurried up the stairs.

Upstairs, a single, small window cast a dim light from the end of a long corridor. Justin groaned when he eyed the double row of wooden doors. *Where to begin?* He started down the dark hall. But his hand was still on the first doorknob when a faint moan drew his eyes to a huddled form on the floor halfway up the corridor. His search was over!

"Mr. Nguyen!" Justin dropped to his knees beside the elderly Vietnamese man. He saw with relief that Danny's grandfather was still alive, but his breathing was fast and shallow. Blood streaked one side of his face. Someone had struck the old man with a heavy blow.

"Mr. Nguyen! What happened?" Mr. Nguyen's eyelids fluttered open.

"Hue . . . tried to stop them . . . I fell." The old man's voice was only a whisper. Turning his head, he gasped, "Danny?"

"He's outside!" Justin slipped an arm under Mr. Nguyen's shoulders. "And we've got to get out of here fast! The Dragon Tong's going to torch the building!"

Justin tried to lift the elderly man to a sitting position, but Mr. Nguyen gave such a moan of pain that he laid him gently back. Glancing down, he saw that the old man's right foot was swollen grotesquely. Justin's stomach knotted. How in the world was he to get the old man out if he couldn't walk?

Lifting a weak hand, Mr. Nguyen clutched at Justin's arm. "You cannot help me. You must save yourself!"

Justin shook his head stubbornly. "No! I'm not leaving you here." He broke off as a man's voice floated up the open stairwell. His heart gave a sickening jolt.

"Go!" Mr. Nguyen ordered feebly. The old man tried to sit up, but with a cry of pain, he fell back against the hardwood floor. Justin heard footsteps and scrambled for the nearest door to hide.

Leaving the door open just a crack, he pressed one eye to the slit. He was almost relieved to see Hue striding down the long corridor. Even if it meant the old man's capture, at least Hue was strong enough to carry Mr. Nguyen downstairs and out of danger. Then Justin would have only himself to get out.

But the Dragon Tong leader made no attempt to help. Instead he gave the old man a rough nudge with one foot. Then with a low, satisfied laugh, Hue ran lightly back down the hall and disappeared.

Justin saw the lighted match spiral through the air a split second before it hit the floor. He threw open the door of the room and grabbed Mr. Nguyen under the armpits. A sheet of flame raced down the trail of spilled gasoline! Dragging the old man inside the room, Justin slammed the door just as it roared past.

Justin lowered the old man to the floor. His heart thudded against his chest. He drew in a deep breath, trying to calm down enough to think. Then he looked around.

The small room was empty except for a twin-sized iron bedstead with an old-fashioned spring mattress. A worn rubber floor mat with the faded word *Welcome* lay beside the bed.

Smoke curled under the door, and Justin choked as the acrid smell caught in his throat. Pulling his jacket over his nose and mouth, he rushed across the room to the large window. Stripping off his jacket, he wrapped it around his fist and struck the window a hard blow. The glass shattered and Justin gasped with relief as fresh air rushed in.

He knocked out the rest of the glass and leaned out. He didn't bother shouting for help. The only ones to hear were the Dragon Tong, and Justin knew now that Hue was perfectly willing to see Mr. Nguyen—and Justin, too—trapped by the fire. *It's like Danny said. Hue won't commit murder, but he'll sure let the fire take care of things for him!*

Justin looked down. To his left, he saw a drainpipe. The metal tubing ran down from the roof right next to the window

He eyed the metal tubing. If it would hold his weight, he could shinny down the pipe and make his way over to the second-story window. From there, he could look for a safe way to the ground. But it would mean leaving Mr. Nguyen to certain death, since there was no way he could bring help before the fire broke through the door and swept over the room.

Pulling his head back inside, Justin saw that billows of smoke were thickening the air despite the open window. He hurried across the room, pausing to give the old man a worried glance. Danny's grandfather was beginning to stir.

Justin had learned enough about fire safety to know better than to open the door. But he ran a quick hand over the solid wood. The heat under his hand and the crackling outside told him that the gas-soaked floorboards of the hall were well on fire. It was only a matter of time before the flames ate through the heavy wood of the door.

What I need is a rope! Then I could lower Mr. Nguyen out the window. There were no bed linens or curtains in the room, but Justin yanked his T-shirt over his head. Ripping it open, he tied the length of torn cloth to one sleeve of his jacket. Pulling off his shoes, he did the same with his socks. But this gave him only a few scant feet of rope. He knelt beside Mr. Nguyen. The elderly Vietnamese moaned and opened his eyes as Justin raised him just enough to slip off the cardigan sweater he was wearing.

Justin gasped. A tiny spurt of flame was creeping under the door and across the wooden floor! Grabbing the rubber floor mat, he rolled it up and stuffed it against the door. If it would only hold the fire out for a few more minutes!

Justin added the cardigan, then his belt to his makeshift rope. Tugging on the heavy metal bedstead, he pulled and pushed it until the headboard was hard against the window. Then he tied the knotted bundle of clothing to the headboard and tossed it out the window.

To his dismay the makeshift rope reached barely a third of the way down the side of the building. By the time he secured the rope under Mr. Nguyen's armpits, there would be little length left.

The smoke was getting worse! Justin coughed and rubbed at his streaming eyes. *If we just had a safety net like the firemen use!* His eye fell on the twin mattress on which he was kneeling. Maybe he could lower Mr. Nguyen, then drop him onto the mattress.

Scrambling down from the iron bedstead, Justin shoved a shoulder against the edge of the mattress. But the mattress was an old-fashioned box spring with a heavy steel frame. Though he strained and tugged, he wasn't strong enough to lift the mattress to the windowsill. Besides, he realized with despair, even if he *had* managed to drop the mattress, he couldn't lower the old man through the window alone.

The fire had not yet reached the closed bedrooms of the third floor. But flames of red and orange were now licking at most of the other windows. Justin was wondering frantically what to do next when an explosion knocked him off his feet. Grabbing at the windowsill, he saw a ball of blue flame burst through the back door. *The gas stove!*

Glancing back into the room, Justin saw that Mr. Nguyen was now fully conscious. He had pulled himself to a sitting position and was leaning against the wall, clutching at his chest as he coughed. The old man made a feeble motion with one hand. Through the haze of smoke, Justin saw him mouth the word, "Go!"

Justin looked down again. The makeshift rope reached almost

to the second story. If he climbed down to the end of the rope and jumped, there was some chance he would get off with only broken bones.

Or he could use the same rope to swing across to the drainpipe. Either plan would mean abandoning Mr. Nguyen to the fire. But it looked now as though neither would make it!

I can't just leave him! But what can I do? He shut his eyes, slumping exhausted against the bedstead. *Dear God, You've got to help me think of a way!*

His head ached badly and in spite of his prayer, panic squeezed at his chest. *If I just had a little more time!*

But even as he turned, he knew there was no more time for him or Mr. Nguyen. A small trail of flame was licking up the inside frame of the wooden door that alone stood between them and the crackling furnace on the other side!

Chapter Thirteen

A FOILED ESCAPE

"Justin! Where are you?"

Justin's first thought was that he had imagined his sister's voice.

"Ju-u-u-stin!"

Was Jenny calling outside? He thrust his head through the window. His sister stood in the parking lot three stories below, staring with horror at the burning building. "Jenny!" he gasped. "Up here!"

Jenny glanced around as though searching for his voice. Cupping his hands around his mouth, Justin called again, "Jenny! I'm up here!"

Jenny looked up. With an exclamation of relief and dismay she ran to stand under his window. "Oh, Justin!" she wailed.

"Hurry, Jenny! I can't get Mr. Nguyen out!" Justin motioned toward the drainpipe. "Maybe you could climb up there. Then I'll throw you the rope!"

But Jenny had already grasped his predicament. Before he had finished speaking, she shinnied up the drainpipe.

"Oof! Ouch! It's hot!" she panted, gripping the square, metal sides of the pipe between her legs and pulling herself upward.

Justin glanced back inside the room. The flames were

spreading up the door frame. Mr. Nguyen had dragged himself over to the door and was using the rolled-up floor mat to beat at the flames. But already a small tongue of fire had caught at the top of the wooden door. Their time was growing short!

Justin turned back to the window. It didn't take long for Jenny, an expert on the ropes in the school gym, to climb the pipe. When she reached a point parallel to the window, he tossed her one end of the bundle of knotted clothes. Wrapping her legs tightly around the metal tubing, she leaned out at a precarious angle to reach for the rope.

It took several tries before she caught the rope. When she did, the force of her grab yanked her free from the drainpipe, sending her spinning and slamming her hard against the side of the brick building. Justin held his breath, sure that the blow had shaken her loose. But Jenny, swinging pendulum-style below the window, clung doggedly to the rope.

"Pull me up, Justin, before I fall!" she called up crossly.

It took all Justin's strength to haul her up to the window. "Where's Mr. Nguyen?" She gasped as she caught sight of the old man's blood-streaked face. "What happened?"

"Later!" Justin grunted. "Help me lift this!"

He was already struggling with the heavy mattress, and Jenny hurried to help him. Together they lifted the mattress to the windowsill. It was a narrow fit, but with much grunting and shoving, they managed to push it through the window. Justin gave a sigh of satisfaction as he saw it land directly below the window.

"Now! Your coat and socks!" He was already pulling off Jenny's jacket. He hauled up the makeshift rope while his sister stripped off her shoes and socks. Knotting Jenny's additions to the end of the rope, he asked, "Did you ever get through to Lieutenant Adams?"

Jenny nodded. "He'd already gotten our message. He's on his way." Glancing around the smoke-filled room, she added dryly, "He also said to stay out of trouble until he got here."

Justin didn't answer. Tugging the last knot tight, he called, "Mr. Nguyen! We'd better get out of here, now!"

Mr. Nguyen had managed to pull himself to one foot. He was still beating feebly at the flames, but despite his efforts, the fire had spread up the edges of the door. Jenny hurried to help him hobble over to the window.

Justin slid the rope under the old man's armpits. "We'll lower you down as far as we can, then drop you onto the mattress."

"So how do *we* get down?" Jenny threw an anxious glance at the flames that were now licking uncontrollably at the door frame and beginning to eat into the hardwood boards of the floor. "If we drop the rope with Mr. Nguyen . . ."

Justin looked out the window, dismayed. Even now, the rope would hardly reach to the first story. Mr. Nguyen would not be able to untie the rope around his chest while swinging almost ten feet above the ground. Jenny was right! They would have to drop the rope. His mind raced frantically. Could Mr. Nguyen toss the rope back up? Maybe he and Jenny could somehow reach the drainpipe. But he knew there was no time!

"No! This is not necessary!" Mr. Nguyen was pushing Justin's hands away. Grabbing the rope away from Justin, he rapidly knotted a sock at one end into a small loop. "I will put my foot in here. I will hold to the rope while you let me down."

"But you aren't well. You'll fall!" Justin protested even as he realized that this was the only solution.

"I will not fall!" The old man's voice was weak but firm. He gasped with pain as he tried to pull himself to the windowsill. "It is the only way!"

Justin and Jenny hurried to help the old man up. Sliding his good foot into the loop, Mr. Nguyen twisted his gnarled hands around the rope and slid over the edge of the windowsill. Even with the open window, the smoke and heat were now almost unbearable, and both twins were choked and blinked away tears as they lowered the elderly man toward the ground.

When they had played out all the rope, they waited in agony as Mr. Nguyen carefully maneuvered his foot loose and lowered himself hand by hand down the remaining few feet of rope. Justin was shoving Jenny out the window even before Mr. Nguyen released the rope. He saw the old man land with a grunt of pain in the middle of the mattress. Then Justin clambered to the windowsill.

Justin swung himself over the edge just as the entire door crashed in, sending a whoosh of flame across the room. The blast of heat singed his hair as he grabbed for the rope. The makeshift rope creaked ominously under their combined weight, but the knots held, and a moment later he felt Jenny release the rope.

Justin lowered himself as rapidly as he could, but he was only halfway down when a sudden jolt of the rope jerked his attention upward. Flames shot from the window, and he saw with horror that their length of knotted clothing had caught on fire. He slid faster, the rope burning his palms as he let it slip through his hands. He had almost reached the end when the rope broke.

Tumbling backward he landed on the spring mattress with a thud that knocked the air from his lungs.

He lay on his back for several long, gasping breaths of fresh air. He couldn't believe they'd made it out alive! Rolling to a sitting position, he winced as a rusty spring thrust its way through the worn mattress cover and into the seat of his jeans. Yes, he was definitely still alive!

Brushing away the remnants of the rope, Justin looked around for his sister. She had pulled Mr. Nguyen to the far end of the mattress to make room for Justin's fall and was kneeling beside him. The old man looked more battered than ever, his left foot now all shades of purple above the leather slipper, but he sat up.

Wiping sweat and tears from his eyes, Justin stared with awe at the brick restaurant. The Dragon Tong had done their work well. Black smoke mingled with the red and orange flames that now billowed from every opening. The blue of burning natural gas still flickered through the shattered back door.

The thought of the Dragon Tong suddenly reminded Justin of the danger they were still in. Where were the police? He glanced at his watch. He could have sworn he'd spent a lifetime—or at least several hours—trapped in that burning room. But to his astonishment, he found that scarcely ten minutes had passed since the fire started.

He sprang to his feet. "Jenny, we've got to get Mr. Nguyen out of here before Hue and his gang show up!"

But it was too late. Even as they slipped their arms under the old man's shoulders to help him to his feet, a now-familiar accent sneered behind them, "You were going somewhere?"

Justin and Jenny eased Mr. Nguyen back, to a sitting position.

Then they straightened up. Slowly they turned around. Hue and two of his followers were standing behind them.

"So! The old man escaped!" Picking up the remnants of Justin's makeshift rope, Hue studied the length of charred clothing. "And you two! Still you are putting your tongue into my business!"

"Nose!" Justin corrected with automatic disdain. He was mildly surprised to discover that he was no longer afraid. He knew he should be. The Dragon Tong leader looked both angry and dangerous. But Justin had been through so many shocks and narrow escapes in the last few hours that he only felt exhausted and a little numb.

"You think you are clever!" Hue took a step forward to loom over the twins. "Perhaps it is true you are clever. Danny told me how you broke down the wall. But only a fool would have come back for this . . ."

The last word was in Vietnamese, but Justin had no trouble guessing what sort of word it was. Hissing another Vietnamese phrase, Hue aimed a contemptuous kick at Mr. Nguyen. White lines of pain tightened around the old man's mouth as Hue jarred his injured foot, but Mr. Nguyen remained silent. Justin clenched his fists with anger. It took all his self-control to keep from hurling himself at that sneering face.

Turning his back on the elderly Vietnamese, the Dragon Tong leader thrust his broad face close to Justin. "Tell me! Did you call the police?"

Justin and Jenny exchanged a quick glance, then tightened their lips stubbornly. Hue's powerful shoulders lifted under the black silk. "It does not matter. They will come soon anyway. But we will be gone!"

The Dragon Tong leader snapped an order to his two followers. One of the masked men yanked Mr. Nguyen to his feet, ignoring the old man's low moan of pain. The other grabbed Jenny by the arm. Hue twisted cruel fingers around Justin's neck.

"You wished to interfere with the business of the Vietnamese," he hissed in his ear. "So you, too, will go with us. Only this time there will be no escape!"

Chapter Fourteen

LIEUTENANT ADAMS

Justin no longer had the will to even think of escape. From the corner of his eye, he saw his sister, her chin still tilted rebelliously but tears spilling down her cheeks. *Where are you, Lieutenant Adams?* he wondered hopelessly.

"Come! We must go!" Hue prodded Justin forward. He stumbled and would have fallen but for the vicious grip on the back of his neck. He had hardly recovered his balance when a black-and-white police sedan raced around the corner of the empty lot and into the street behind the restaurant. Bumping over the curb, it screeched to a stop only a few yards away.

Hue whirled around, releasing Justin so fast that he almost fell again. Justin felt the man's powerful muscles tense to flee, but four uniformed police officers were already slamming out of the car and taking cover behind the police vehicle. Four deadly looking assault rifles appeared over the top of the car. Then a loudspeaker blasted, "This is the police! Stay where you are and put your hands in the air!"

Hue slowly lifted his hands above his head. The other two Dragon Tong members had also released their captives and were sidling off to the left, but a quick gesture from their leader brought them to a stop. They too raised their hands in the air.

Justin felt like letting out a triumphant yell. Lieutenant Adams had come through after all! *You did it again, God!* he breathed. *Thanks!* Backing out of the Dragon Tong leader's reach, he hurried over to his sister. "Are you okay?" he whispered.

Jenny sniffed, running the back of her hand across her soot-and-tear-streaked face. "Yeah, I'm fine. But Mr. Nguyen looks pretty bad."

Mr. Nguyen did look in bad shape. He was swaying on his good foot, his eyes shut and his thin face gray. Justin hurried to slip his shoulder under one arm while Jenny supported his other side. Together, they helped Mr. Nguyen to a sitting position, his injured leg stretched out in front of him. The elderly man murmured his thanks, but he kept his eyes shut.

Sergeant Preston and Officer Rodriguez broke cover. They strode across the pavement toward the small group, the other two police officers backing them up with their rifles from the police car.

The wiry Officer Rodriguez drew a pistol from a hip holster and circled around behind the three members of the Dragon Tong. Hue, who had removed his face mask, met the big Sergeant Preston's eyes with a cold look. His own gun held skyward, Sergeant Preston reached out and ripped the hoods off the other two men's faces. Justin couldn't suppress a sudden shiver at the naked hatred on their faces as they emerged from the silk covering.

Sergeant Preston glanced over at the teenagers, then ordered brusquely, "Get away from the kids!" He motioned with his gun for the three men to move to one side.

Hue, his followers at his heels, walked with calm dignity to the spot the police sergeant indicated. Officer Rodriguez circled behind the three men, keeping them covered. But Hue made no attempt to escape, and he kept his hands well above his head. "You are making a mistake!" he said, in his heavily accented English. "We have done nothing."

"Sure! No one ever does!" Officer Rodriguez snapped. He prodded Hue in the back with his gun. "On the ground and spread your legs."

Hue swung around, his wide nostrils flaring with fury. But after a considering glance at Officer Rodriguez' furious eyes and the gun in his hand, he snapped a phrase in Vietnamese. Dropping face down to the ground, the three men spread their arms and legs apart. The officer patted up and down both sides of their bodies. He grunted with satisfaction as he removed a knife from each of the men's costumes.

"They're armed, all right!" he called to Sergeant Preston.

Sergeant Preston nodded, then walked over to Justin and Jenny. "So it's you two again," he growled. "I might have known!" His eyes narrowed as he took in their filthy condition. "You look like you've been through a war!" Pulling out a huge, snowy handkerchief, he handed it to Jenny. "Here. I'd say you need this more than I do."

Jenny managed a small smile as she took the handkerchief and blew her nose. "We told you there really was a Dragon Tong." She waved a hand toward the snarling red-and-gold dragons on the backs of the three men spread-eagled on the ground. "They're the ones who set the building on fire!"

"Yeah? Well, I guess you were telling the truth after all," the burly police officer admitted with an unwilling grin. He looked past the twins to Mr. Nguyen. Taking in the old man's blood-streaked face and swollen foot, he raised his voice to a bellow. "Smith, looks like we need an ambulance here!"

"No! No!" Mr. Nguyen opened his eyes as one of the other police officers hurried over. "I must find my grandson!"

"Danny Nguyen," Justin explained to the two officers. "The Dragon Tong had him, too!"

"He's probably safe with Lieutenant Adams by now," Sergeant Preston reassured him. "He's around front rounding up the rest of this gang." Shouts and the sound of a loudspeaker came from the other side of the building. Pointing to the other officer, he said kindly, "We'll make sure your grandson is okay, Mr. Nguyen. Smith here will get you to a hospital."

"No! I am fine! It is only a sprain!" Lines of pain etched the corners of his mouth, but he shook his head stubbornly. "I will go nowhere until I see my grandson."

"Well, if you're sure that's what you want." Sergeant Preston gave a reluctant nod to the other policeman. "Smith, you and Hansen take this gentleman and the kids around to Lieutenant Adams. Rodriguez and I'll be along in a minute."

The officer named Smith eased Mr. Nguyen into the back of the police car. The twins climbed in next to the driver. As the car circled the burning building, Justin saw that both ends of the street in front of the restaurant were cordoned off. At each end of the block, a pair of police sedans were pulled tightly against the curb, their overhead blue and red lights flashing in rhythm. Justin counted at least a dozen blue uniforms moving about.

"Wow! I guess they took us seriously this time," he whispered in Jenny's ear as they pulled up to the police barrier.

"Look! There's Lieutenant Adams!" Jenny pointed out the lieutenant standing beside one of the police cars just ahead. Jenny scrambled out of the car before it had fully stopped.

"We'll find Danny for you," Justin reassured Mr. Nguyen hurriedly. Then he took off after his sister.

Lieutenant Adams was giving orders to two of his men when the twins ran up behind him. "I want all possible witnesses out here where we can question them," Justin heard him say. "And keep an eye out for those kids!"

The tall lieutenant swung around at the sound of the twins' footsteps. "Oh, there you are. I was getting worried!" He raised an incredulous eyebrow. "What happened to you two? I thought I told you to stay out of trouble!"

Justin had forgotten that he was minus half his clothes. He brushed self-consciously at the soot and plaster that streaked his bare chest. "They left Mr. Nguyen inside. We had to get him out!"

"Who left who *where?* Kids, I think you've got some explaining to do!" The tall lieutenant sounded severe, but his warm smile showed how pleased he was to see them.

"Well, you see, we were just . . . ," Justin started. But just then he caught sight of a row of black figures spread-eagled against a nearby wall. Their hoods were pulled down, and two policemen were searching them while two others covered the group with assault rifles. Justin counted the men. *Let's see! That's five of the Dragon Tong here plus Hue and the other two Sergeant Preston and Officer Frank arrested.* "Hey, you got all of them!" he exclaimed.

"That's because when I called, I told him to leave the sirens off," his sister informed him with smug satisfaction. "So the Dragon Tong wouldn't hear them and get away like last time!"

Lieutenant Adams ruffled her dark curls. "Thanks for the tip, Jenny! I'm sure we wouldn't have thought of it without you."

"Hey, Lieutenant Adams!" Justin was looking around, his freckled face anxious. "Where's Danny?"

"Danny?" One of Lieutenant Adam's eyebrows shot up. "Who's Danny?"

"Our Vietnamese friend—the one we told you about." Justin turned in a complete circle to search for his friend. "The Dragon Tong had him; Sergeant Preston said he'd be with you."

Lieutenant Adams shook his head. "I'm sorry, kids. The men we captured weren't holding any hostage. They must have let him go when they saw us coming."

He nodded toward the police cordon. "I told my men to round up everyone in sight. Maybe you'll find your friend in the crowd somewhere."

He broke off as a sudden shrill whine announced an approaching fire engine. The police cordon was hastily lifted aside. Racing down the street, the elongated red truck screeched to a halt in front of the restaurant. Firemen in yellow coats jumped down and began unloading hoses.

Another fire engine, this one a hook-and-ladder truck, screamed around the corner to the back of the restaurant. The blaze across the wide street was now belching smoke and ashes high into the air.

"Excuse me, kids. I need to talk to the fire chief." Lieutenant Adams strode across the street.

Justin and Jenny hurried over to the police cordon to look for Danny. A small crowd of Vietnamese was beginning to spill onto the sidewalk as shoppers and others who had taken refuge in the nearest store were escorted outside. Police officers waved them back from the fire department's activity. Leaning over the barrier, Justin and Jenny scanned the jostling, protesting crowd.

"There he is!" Jenny exclaimed. Following her pointing finger, Justin saw a small, forlorn figure sitting on a curb, watching listlessly as the enormous jets of water began to sizzle against the shooting flames.

"Danny!" he called. "Over here!"

Danny's head came up with a jerk. His eyes widened as he caught sight of the twins waving from behind the barrier. Jumping to his feet, he pushed through the crowd. Justin and Jenny slipped under the police cordon to meet him.

Danny's round face was tear-streaked. Giving both of them a fierce hug, he gulped, "I thought you'd been caught inside. I should never have asked you to go!" His anxious gaze shifted past Justin's shoulder. "Where's *Ông Nôi?* You . . . you *did* find him?"

"It's OK, Danny. We got him out!" Justin gestured back to where Mr. Nguyen leaned heavily on the arm of a police officer and limped toward the police cordon. With a cry of gladness, Danny sprinted toward his grandfather.

The twins followed more slowly. They were introducing Danny and Mr. Nguyen to Lieutenant Adams when they saw Sergeant Preston and Officer Frank herd Hue and his two men toward the police cordon. The officers were watchful, and they kept their weapons trained on the three Dragon Tong members.

Jenny tugged at Lieutenant Adams' sleeve. "That's the leader of the Dragon Tong."

"Yeah!" Justin added, giving Hue a dark look. "He's the one who knocked out Mr. Nguyen and left him to die!"

The two patrol officers were shoving Hue and his two followers in with the rest of the Dragon Tong when a young officer approached Lieutenant Adams. He waved a hand toward the crowd of twenty or thirty Vietnamese store owners and shoppers who had gathered on the sidewalk. "None of them seem to have seen anything!" he said with frustration. "Do you want us to move them out of here?"

"Not just yet," Lieutenant Adams ordered. "Let's see if we can get someone to identify some of this bunch." He turned to the police officer who had given the twins and Mr. Nguyen a ride. "Smith, why don't you find Mr. Nguyen a chair. Then see if you can get a paramedic over here."

While Officer Smith hurried off to bring a chair from a nearby store, Lieutenant Adams strode toward the crowd. Danny and the twins helped Mr. Nguyen hobble over to sit near the other store owners and shoppers. As Justin settled the old man into the chair, he recognized several people. There was the grocery store owner, Mrs. Trinh, at the back, holding a small, pale boy by the hand. There were even some of the regular customers he'd seen in the restaurant.

Lieutenant Adams signaled the officers who were guarding the Dragon Tong to bring the prisoners forward. Faint hisses and murmurs of recognition swept the small crowd of Vietnamese as they caught sight of the men's unmasked features. There was anger in their faces, but fear and shock were uppermost, and they glanced away to avoid meeting the unrepentant glares of the Dragon Tong members.

Despite his handcuffs and the police guards at his back, Hue managed to look both arrogant and dangerous. Without waiting to be questioned, he stepped forward. "Why have you treated me and my men with such shame?" he demanded. "We have done nothing wrong! Why do you treat us like criminals?"

"You've done nothing wrong?" Lieutenant Adams repeated dryly. He flicked a finger at the black silk that covered Hue from head to foot. "Then maybe you can tell us what you are doing here dressed like that. And how this fire started!"

Hue shrugged, his powerful muscles rippling visibly under the black silk. "My friends and I are learning what you call 'martial arts'. We were practicing the Vietnamese way of fighting when we heard screams and shouting. When we saw that a fire had started, we came to help rescue those caught inside."

"That's a lie!" Jenny gasped, outraged. "You started the fire! And you left Mr. Nguyen inside to burn!"

Hue ignored her outburst. His hooded gaze traveled across the crowd of Vietnamese. "You have only to ask my neighbors here. They will tell you how we came to help."

There was a shuffling of feet and flickering sideways glances, but no one contradicted Hue's statements. Justin waited for Mr. Nguyen to deny the Dragon Tong leader's outrageous lies, but the old man sat in silence, his eyes fastened on the pavement beneath his chair.

"He's so conceited!" Jenny whispered indignantly to her twin. "He's so sure no one's brave enough to tell the truth about him."

"Maybe he's right," Justin whispered back soberly. He turned his attention back to Lieutenant Adams.

"Are you denying that you are the leader of the 'Dragon Tong'?" the tall police lieutenant asked.

"The Dragon Tong?" Hue scoffed. "It is but a story! A name given by children because of the dragon on our backs. We wear these clothes only to practice fighting."

"Yeah? And you always wear masks when you rescue people from burning buildings?" Sergeant Preston added.

Hue's gaze shifted to the burly sergeant. "It was to keep the smoke out."

The answer was so unexpected that Justin had to suppress a giggle and several of the police officers snickered openly. Lieutenant Adams raised a hand for silence. Motioning to the gathered crowd, he said sternly, "You have been accused of extorting money from these Vietnamese business owners. It was reported that you were seen starting this fire."

"By these children, I am sure!" Hue's guttural tones were contemptuous, but the twitch of his left eye betrayed his anger. "These two have been making trouble since they first came to my cousin's home."

He was interrupted as a young officer hurried up. His uniform was streaked with soot, and sweat dotted his forehead despite the cool September breeze. "Look what we found in the alley!" he announced, holding up one of the red gas containers the Dragon Tong had used to start the fire. "And the building was soaked with gasoline. It's arson, all right!"

"Perhaps we can help with this," Hue offered. His white teeth now gleamed in an ingratiating smile. "My friends and I saw some teenage boys running away when we came to help with the fire. They were outsiders, not Vietnamese. It may be that *they* started the fire!"

He waved a black-gloved hand at the listening Vietnamese. "If you ask these others, they may have seen them too."

"Sure they've seen 'em!" Justin muttered angrily to Jenny and Danny. "If Hue says they have."

But Officer Rodriguez nodded agreement. "We *have* been having trouble with a teenage gang in this neighborhood. They trashed the grocery store here just a few days ago."

Justin couldn't believe his ears. "That's not true!" he burst out, pushing his way in front of the wiry patrol officer. "You know there was no gang! The Dragon Tong trashed that store, *and* they burned Mr. Nguyen's restaurant. We saw them!"

He swung around to search the crowd. Yes, there was one of the lunch customers he had seen the Dragon Tong drag from the restaurant, a young Vietnamese man holding a small boy. "You! You were there! They set the restaurant on fire, didn't they?"

The young father clutched his son close, his dark eyes darting sideways toward the Dragon Tong leader. Shaking his head agitatedly he took his wife by the arm and disappeared into the back of the crowd. Justin's shoulders sagged with disappointment. Hue was right! The Vietnamese were even more afraid of the Dragon Tong leader now that they knew who he was.

Lieutenant Adams let out a sigh. Turning to the crowd, he raised his voice. "Okay! I know some of you saw what happened here. Do we have to take you into the police station to make you talk?"

There were more sideways glances, but no one spoke up. Hue,

his arms folded across his powerful chest, gave a satisfied nod as the silence stretched on. Then a man stepped forward. It was the stocky middle-aged Vietnamese man who ran the jewelry shop.

"It is as this man says," he said in slow English. "We saw this man and his friends come to stop the fire. And we saw the boys he speaks of. Of what these children have said, we know nothing!"

The jewelry shop owner looked around at the rest of the crowd. Several nodded agreement.

Officer Rodriguez walked over, his narrow face hard with suspicion. "You two sure manage to be around every time something happens down here! Maybe *you* belong to this gang they've been telling us about."

Lieutenant Adams waved him back with a curt hand motion. "You're way off base, Rodriguez! I've known these kids for years. They're telling the truth."

He looked down at Mr. Nguyen. The old man sat straight in his chair, seemingly giving little attention to the loud conversation. Gesturing toward Hue and the other Dragon Tong members, Lieutenant Adams said with gentle courtesy. "Mr. Nguyen, Justin and Jenny have told me how these men have been stealing your money. Maybe *you* could tell us what happened here today."

Hue's black eyes glittered with fury. His left eyelid was twitching dangerously as he hissed a vicious phrase in Vietnamese. Danny gasped. "He says he will kill us both if *Ông Nôi* does not agree with his story!" he whispered to the twins.

Hue raised his voice to be heard by the rest of the Vietnamese.

A murmur of fear swept the crowd. Danny couldn't keep a tremble from his voice as he translated, "He says, 'I myself will give a terrible death to the one who speaks against the Dragon Tong!'"

"But he's already tried to kill you," Justin whispered back. "Do you really think he'll leave you alone if you back him up now? The only way you're going to be safe is if he's in jail!"

Danny didn't answer, but he knelt beside his grandfather's chair. "Please, *Ông Nội,*" he urged. "You must tell the police. Don't worry about me!"

Jenny knelt on his other side. "Please do what Lieutenant Adams says," she pleaded. "He's our friend. He'll help you."

Mr. Nguyen sat as unmoving as the small bronze Buddha now destroyed in the flames. Only his dark eyes flickered across the unmasked faces of the Dragon Tong. His gaze paused at Hue's openly triumphant sneer. Then he looked down at his kneeling grandson. He placed a gentle hand on Danny's head, but he said nothing.

"So!" Hue's arrogant stare traveled around the circle of watchful police officers to end at Lieutenant Adams. "You will now release me and my friends. As you can see, we have done nothing but try to help an ungrateful neighbor!"

Lieutenant Adams stared back at the big Vietnamese with cold dislike. The tall police lieutenant appeared as calm and under control as always, but Justin noticed his right fist clenching and unclenching. "What I see," he answered in a hard, flat tone, "is that you are guilty as sin—no matter how much you've frightened these people into backing up your story!"

Lieutenant Adams turned to the group. "Don't you

understand?" he demanded, anger edging his voice. "These men are criminals! They've terrorized your businesses and your homes. Isn't there one of you willing to stand up and testify? To put these men behind bars where they belong?"

Another murmur swept the crowd and there was a shuffling of feet. Justin saw fear in their faces, but there was anger and shame there, too. If only someone could rouse that anger against the Dragon Tong. Justin felt like screaming with frustration.

Jenny tugged on Lieutenant Adams' sleeve. "You *are* going to arrest them, aren't you? I mean, you caught them in the act!"

Lieutenant Adams shook his head slowly. "Kids, all the police can testify to is that we found these men and others outside a burning building. They didn't even resist arrest. We can do nothing without proof. We *must* have witnesses."

Glancing down at Mr. Nguyen, he said gently, "Is there nothing at all you have to say, Mr. Nguyen?"

The old man raised his eyes to the Dragon Tong leader, an unreadable expression on his thin face. A triumphant smile spread across Hue's thick lips.

Lieutenant Adams looked sadly down at Justin and Jenny, "I'm sorry, kids. If everyone here is going to back up his story, I have no choice but to release him and his men."

He raised his hand to give the release order. Several of the officers stepped forward to unlock the handcuffs. Justin and Jenny looked at each other in dismay as the restraints dropped away from Hue's wrists. After all that had happened, the Dragon Tong was getting away again.

Chapter Fifteen

STANDING TOGETHER

"No! Do not release them!"

The soft words dropped into a stunned silence, erasing Hue's triumphant sneer. Lowering his hand, Lieutenant Adams turned around slowly. "What did you say?"

"Do not let them go. I will speak." It was Mr. Nguyen. They spun around to stare at the old man, their dismay changing to wonder. Jenny gave Justin's arm an excited squeeze as Danny's grandfather struggled to his feet.

"I have been wrong!" Mr. Nguyen looked ill and frail, but his voice gathered strength as he went on. "My son and my family have bravely faced men who would terrify even the Dragon Tong! But I . . . I have been afraid—afraid for my grandson, for my home. My son would be ashamed of me."

Pulling himself straight in spite of his injured foot, Mr. Nguyen looked across at Hue, his lined, old face suddenly alive with anger and contempt. "You! I have given you a home! A job! But you . . . you have destroyed my home. You have threatened my grandson. And I have been afraid to speak. But no more! It is time to stand—to fight this evil!"

Mr. Nguyen turned to Lieutenant Adams. "I have been afraid long enough. I will speak of what these men have done."

"Me too!" Danny sprang to his grandfather's side, his black eyes sparking with triumph. He glared at Hue. "I'm not afraid of the Dragon Tong. I'll testify!"

Hue stared at Mr. Nguyen with the blank astonishment of a lion whose rabbit prey has suddenly turned on him. He snarled viciously in Vietnamese. Danny took a quick step backward, but Mr. Nguyen only turned his back on the Dragon Tong leader.

"Will we sit here like dogs while these men destroy us one by one?" Mr. Nguyen's voice rang out strong over the crowd. He switched to Vietnamese. Neither the twins nor the police officers understood a word, but the gathered Vietnamese gave startled attention to the old man.

Hue took a long, furious step toward Mr. Nguyen. But suddenly there were several officers barring his way. He shouted in Vietnamese at the crowd, but Mr. Nguyen's voice soared above the Dragon Tong leader's angry curses.

"He says that the Dragon Tong promised to leave us in peace if we would pay," Danny whispered to the twins, who had moved quietly over beside him. "But today they have destroyed our restaurant. Only the help of foreigners—that's you!—saved his life and the life of his grandson—that's me! He says these men are without honor. If we do not stop them, they will destroy us all."

Danny's black eyes shone with pride as he listened to his grandfather. "He is telling them that they too must speak to put these men in jail. He says that the Dragon Tong is a shame to our people—that we lose face before our city because we permit such men in our neighborhood."

There were scattered nods and murmurs of agreement across

the crowd. Justin saw sudden hope struggling with the fear and anger in the dark faces.

"He is telling them that this is America," Danny translated. "That here we don't have to give in to such evil men, that in America the police are here to help us."

The twins exchanged delighted glances as they heard their own words repeated. "If the Vietnamese stand together today," Danny finished, "we can destroy the power of the Dragon Tong forever!"

No one moved for a long moment after the old man's voice trailed off. Even the Dragon Tong members seemed uncertain what to do next, and the only sound was the shouted orders of the firemen across the street. Justin held his breath. *Please, God! You've got to let someone move!*

Then he saw Mrs. Trinh leave her son and thread her way to the front of the crowd. She didn't stop until she stood beside Mr. Nguyen. "I will speak too," she said, in a voice hardly above a whisper. "I will not pay these men anymore."

Hue was now screaming with rage, and the remaining Vietnamese looked at each other nervously. Then, to Justin's surprise and delight, the young couple who had been lunch customers when the Dragon Tong attacked, moved from their hiding place in the crowd.

"For my son I will speak!" The young father clutched the small boy tightly, but his thin face was resolute. "In this America, he must not grow up afraid!"

It was as though the young man's statement had unstopped a dam. The remaining Vietnamese began to crowd forward. Soon only a small knot were left surrounding the scowling jewelry shop owner. Tears stung Justin's eyes. He noticed Jenny was already

143

crying unashamedly. *They did follow Mr. Nguyen,* Justin thought, dazed. *Just like Danny said!*

Hue's broad, dark face was twisted with hatred. With a shriek of rage, he lunged for Mr. Nguyen. There was a sudden flurry of movement, then Hue lay groaning on the concrete pavement. Breathing just a little hard, Lieutenant Adams bent over the Dragon Tong leader and snapped handcuffs around his wrists. The other Dragon Tong members moved restlessly, glancing at each other with angry mutters. But they subsided as a dozen police officers closed in around them, weapons held ready in rock-steady hands.

Lieutenant Adams took time to give them a thumbs-up sign of victory before he turned with a broad smile to his police officers. "Read them their rights and take them away!"

Danny let out a whoop of triumph. Justin and Jenny hugged each other, then Danny and Mr. Nguyen and even Mrs. Trinh. The police officers began recuffing the tong members. Above Hue's steady cursings and a babble of excitement and relief in Vietnamese and English, the deep drawl of Sergeant Preston rang out with grim satisfaction: "You have the right to remain silent. You have a right to a lawyer. Anything you say can and will be used against you in a court of law."

"It was your children who made me speak," Mr. Nguyen told Mom and Dad several hours later. An enormous white bandage circled his head, but the bloodstains had been washed away, and he had changed to some clean, much-too-large clothing from Dad's closet.

"When they risked their lives to save me, I knew they must be telling the truth about the American police. That these policemen *would* help us against the Dragon Tong."

Danny, Justin, and Jenny, also clean and in fresh clothing, had made themselves comfortable on the carpet in the Parker's living room. Mr. Nguyen was stretched out on the sofa, his foot—now in a cast—propped on a pile of cushions. Once the Dragon Tong members had been handcuffed and taken away, Mr. Nguyen had consented to be taken to the emergency room at the nearest hospital. The X-rays had shown his foot to be broken, not just sprained.

Justin looked over at his parents. "I guess we should have told you before we started following Hue around. But we honestly didn't think there was going to be any danger. We just wanted to make sure we were right about Hue before we said anything."

"Yeah, we didn't mean to get into so much trouble," Jenny added, "going into that burning building and all."

Dad stretched out in his armchair. "I'll admit that following Hue wasn't the wisest thing to do, though I appreciate your motives." He laced his fingers behind his head, his freckled face thoughtful. "But I really don't see that you had any choice when it came to going in after Mr. Nguyen."

Justin and Jenny exchanged a startled glance. Really, Dad said the most unexpected things sometimes!

"I thought you'd be mad at us?" Justin's tone was a question.

Dad smiled at their surprise. "Kids, there are too many people who are willing to look the other way when someone's in trouble because they don't want to stick out their own necks. As a parent, it makes me shudder to think of the danger you two were in today. But I would never ask you to stay out of trouble just to save yourselves. You risked your lives to help a friend, and I'm proud of you."

Dad brought the easy chair to an upright position as the phone rang. "Parker residence. Sure! That's great! Yes, I'll let him know."

"That was Doug Adams calling from the police station," he announced when he hung up the receiver. "Hue, of course, has refused to talk. But several of the others have admitted their parts in the protection racket. Through them, the police have managed to recover at least part of the money the gang took from the Vietnamese businesses."

Squeals of joy and hugs followed his announcement. Then Jenny said mournfully, "But you've still lost your restaurant, Mr. Nguyen. What are you and Danny going to do now? I mean, everything you had is gone!"

"They're going to stay right here for now." Mom's gentle tones were firm. "And I'm sure we can work something out."

But Dad and Mr. Nguyen smiled at each other, an astonishingly similar expression of mischief on the two very different faces. "Do not be sad, Jenny," Mr. Nguyen reassured her. "We will soon build again. As with all American businesses, I have insurance on my restaurant."

"What?" All three teenagers sat upright, their mouths dropping open.

"That's right, kids." There was a twinkle in Dad's green eyes. "You wanted to know why Mr. Nguyen talked to me last week. Well, he asked me about insurance for his restaurant, and I helped him set up a policy the very next day."

One reddish-brown eyebrow shot up as he added dryly, "We certainly didn't expect to need it so soon!"

"There's one other thing I don't get," Justin said, when the babble of excited chatter had died down. "About Hue and the rest of the Dragon Tong. I guess I kind of expected to see some karate today. I mean, with those dragon costumes and all."

Danny snorted with disgust. "Americans always think anyone with an Asian face is a martial arts expert. I'll bet Hue doesn't know any more karate than I do."

"Danny's right." Mr. Nguyen's dark eyes smiled at the obvious disappointment on Justin's face. "Only a few in any Asian country are trained in martial arts. Most of my people are too busy trying to survive to spend their time in such training."

He gave Danny a reproving look. "But that does not mean they cannot be good fighters. Hue and his men were all soldiers in Vietnam. They are very dangerous men. Be thankful that this Lieutenant Adams and the American police are also trained fighters!"

Raising himself with a struggle to a sitting position, Mr. Nguyen laid a hand on Danny's shoulder. "I will never be able to repay you for what you have done for me and my grandson," he said softly, his gaze traveling around the four Parkers. "I do not know how to thank you enough!"

The old man pulled out a borrowed handkerchief to polish suddenly damp glasses. Replacing his glasses, he looked down at Justin, who was lying beside Danny at his feet. "Justin, I told you to leave me, but you stayed. What is it about you Christians that you are so eager to risk your lives for others?"

Mr. Nguyen looked across at Mom and Dad. "My friends,

your children have told you of my family—of how they died. But there is one thing I have not told them. That night on the boat when my wife died, she begged me to become a Christian— to give my life to God. She said that she would be waiting to see me in heaven."

The old man's voice broke, and he bowed his head. "All these years I have been angry at the missionaries. But I was really angry at myself. If I had died today, if Justin had not come back for me, I would never have seen my family again. I have fought God enough! I want now to follow Him."

It was much later when Jenny joined the boys in Justin's room to help set up a foldout cot for Danny.

"Oh, by the way, Danny," Justin said, tucking in an over-large sheet. "I forgot to ask. How in the world did you know we were hiding behind that trash bin? I mean, we could tell you were talking to us."

"Easy!" Danny's grin was impish. "I just read your minds! One of those martial arts tricks, you know." He lifted his hands in mock fear as Justin raised a threatening pillow over his head. "Okay! Okay! I was standing at a window just before Hue's men grabbed me, and I saw you guys running down the alley. I knew that's where you'd hide. There was nowhere else."

Danny sobered. "Hey, guys, do you remember those Christian words you told me in the warehouse? You know, the ones about everything working out good?"

Justin lowered the pillow. "You mean, 'And we know that in all things God works for the good of those who love him.'"

"Yeah, that one," Danny nodded. "I think I'm beginning to see what you mean. A few hours ago, I didn't think things could get any worse. We'd lost the restaurant, and for all I knew, my grandfather was gone, too. If someone had asked me, I'd have said nothing good could ever happen out of all that mess. But look now! The Dragon Tong is in jail, and we're going to build an even better restaurant. Chances look pretty good for going to medical school, and *Ông Nôi* is even going to let me learn about being a Christian like my parents!"

He stopped suddenly. "Do you really think *Ông Nôi* and I will see them again someday?"

"I know you will!" Jenny said softly. Her eyes were shining.

Justin swallowed an enormous yawn. "Well, one thing's for sure. With the Dragon Tong out of the way, things are going to seem pretty tame around here!"

"There's still the Devlons," Jenny teased slyly.

"Not with Danny around," Justin retorted, tossing the pillow at his sister. "No, the rest of this year's going to be a breeze!"

He was interrupted by a pillow to the face. But as the small bedroom erupted into an all-out pillow fight, Justin had no idea that the safety of the whole country would soon rest on his shoulders as a web of international espionage plunged the entire Parker family into danger.

PARKER TWINS POWER

Don't Miss Any of These High Octane Adventures

Captured in Colombia

Cave of the Inca Re

Jungle Hideout

Mystery at Death Canyon

Race for the Secret Code

Secret of the Dragon Mark